Roman Empire:

Rise & The Fall. Explore The History, Mythology, Legends, Epic Battles & The Lives Of The Emperors, Legions, Heroes, Gladiators & More

History Brought Alive

© Copyright 2021 - All rights reserved.

The content contained within this book may not be reproduced, duplicated or transmitted without direct written permission from the author or the publisher.

Under no circumstances will any blame or legal responsibility be held against the publisher, or author, for any damages, reparation, or monetary loss due to the information contained within this book, either directly or indirectly.

Legal Notice:

This book is copyright protected. It is only for personal use. You cannot amend, distribute, sell, use, quote or paraphrase any part, or the content within this book, without the consent of the author or publisher.

Disclaimer Notice:

Please note the information contained within this document is for educational and entertainment purposes only. All effort has been executed to present accurate, up to date, reliable, complete information. No warranties of any kind are declared or implied. Readers acknowledge that the author is not engaged in the rendering of legal, financial, medical or professional advice. The content within this book has been derived from various sources. Please consult a licensed professional before attempting any techniques outlined in this book.

By reading this document, the reader agrees that under no circumstances is the author responsible for any losses, direct or indirect, that are incurred as a result of the use of the information contained within this document, including, but not limited to, errors, omissions, or inaccuracies.

Free Bonus From Hba: Ebook Bundle

Greetings!

First of all, thank you for reading our books. As fellow passionate readers of history and mythology we aim to create the very best books for our readers.

Now, we invite you to join our VIP list. As a welcome gift we offer the History & Mythology Ebook Bundle below for free. Plus you can be the first to receive new books and exclusives! Remember it's 100% free to join.

Simply click the link below to join.

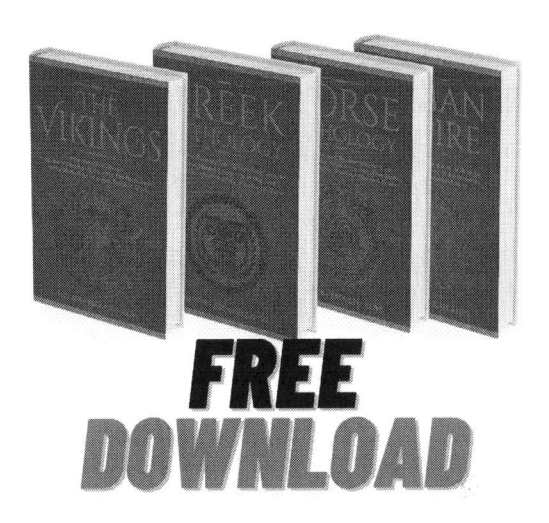

Click Here For Your Free Bonus (https://www.subscribepage.com/hba)

Keep Upto Date With Us On:

YouTube: History Brought Alive
Facebook: History Brought Alive
www.historybroughtalive.com

TABLE OF CONTENTS

Introduction
Chapter 1: Timeline
  The Three Periods of Ancient Rome
  The Time of the Emperors
  The Decline, Invasion, and Fall of Rome
Chapter 2: The Geography of Rome
  Rome's Place in the World
  The Geography of the City
  Roman Roads
Chapter 3: The Main Figures in Roman History
  Political Figures
    Emperors
  Famous Writers
  Poets, Artists, and Musicians
  Famous Military Figures
  Gladiators
Chapter 4: Roman Life
  Roman Food and Cooking
  Roman Jobs
  A Typical Day

Family

School

Clothing

Entertainment

Chapter 5: Mythology

    The Mythological Origin of Rome

    Roman Gods

    Other Cultural Myths

    Paganism in Ancient Rome

Chapter 7: Roman Military

    Structure

    Logistics

    Legions

    Training

    Navy

    Weapons and Tactics

    Famous Battles

Chapter 8: Decline And Fall Of The Roman Empire

    The Beginning Of The End Of The Roman Empire

        Factors That Led to the Empire's Decline

        The Timeline for the Decline

        The Fall of the Empire in 476

        Aftermath

Conclusion

References

INTRODUCTION

Author Bio

History Brought Alive is a company that specializes in writing expertly crafted works on ancient world history and mythology. The books we write are informative, factual, and ideal for anyone wanting to learn more about the past and the world we live in. Our books aim to teach the eager reader, to open your mind, and to challenge your assumptions about history in ways you never thought of before. This book is a timeless reference you will want to use over and over! These lovingly constructed works are written to endure. The legacy they produce will last through the ages and entertain, satisfy and empower generations of readers.

Roma Victrix

In AD 27, an empire was born. A tiny settlement on the banks of the Tiber River developed and grew into a colossal, unstoppable force, a power unrivaled in the ancient world. At its peak, the Roman Empire dominated the world from continental Europe, Britain, Western Asia, North Africa, and many other territories. Modern language, religion, culture, and way of life all sprang forth from this empire. "SPQR" was the motto of the Roman Empire: *Senatus Populusque Romanus* (meaning the Senate and the Roman people). This motto stood for the entirety and inevitability of the Roman state, the two aspects of her greatness: both her people and her government (or Senate). Rome's greatness was not only evident in her military might, but also in her technological advancements, her progressive way of life, and her hegemony over the cultures of the world. At that time, Rome was at the forefront of the advancement of civilization, and her rule was total.

The study of Roman history is vast and complex. We can break the study of Ancient Rome into different areas that will make it easier to analyze. Much like the Ancient Romans themselves, to study this civilization, we have to adhere to the principles of order, structure, and discipline. First, we have the timeline of Roman history. How did it all begin? What were the factors that led to the rise and founding of Rome? What were the factors that led to its eventual decline? Important events are easier to understand if they are enumerated in chronological order. We can view the most important events in Roman history as they occurred, and we can easily see the context surrounding these events.

Next, we have the lay of the land itself. What was

Rome built on, literally? What was the topography and geography of Ancient Rome? Important topics to consider when thinking about the geography of Ancient Rome are the way the mountains surrounding the city played a role in its development. These terrain features weren't only used for the defense of the city and the empire; how the Ancient Romans used the environment also played a role in their development as a civilization. The geography of the region itself was inextricably linked to the culture and the history of the empire.

The characters of Ancient Rome made it what it is, a political and social theatre of intrigue. Much of Roman life centered around the figures in authority at that time. Any serious study has to begin with a look at the emperors themselves. Not only that, but what has to be examined is also the way in which the Senate played its role in the empire. Beyond the nature of government in Ancient Rome, there are the playwrights, wordsmiths, scholars, poets, philosophers, warriors, and the ordinary men and women who made up the empire. Every single one of these people shows a different aspect of Ancient Rome as a whole. They are a microcosm of what the society must have been like, and their stories are fascinating to behold. The beating heart of Ancient Rome was its people.

How did Romans survive in everyday life? Roman life became amongst the most advanced of any civilization anywhere in the world. Rome was the educated world, the civilized world and the beacon of light people saw in an otherwise dark and uncivilized society. Rome survived because it implemented a way of life that was successful for everyone in the society at the time. The rigidity of the society as a whole bred a sense of duty and patriotism towards the empire and to Rome herself. People knew what was expected of them on any given day. Loyalty was the currency of the realm. The Roman way of life was structured in such a way that the civilization as a whole, thrived and grew.

When people think of Rome, they think about the military first and foremost; and with good reason. The Roman military was amongst the most powerful in the world. How did they get that way? From a small army of men to one of the greatest fighting forces the world has ever seen, the Roman army was the gold standard for centuries because of their discipline, dedication, ruthlessness, and skill. Backed up by a thorough training regimen, Roman soldiers were considered to be amongst the best in the world at what they did. And what they did was to conquer the known world and spill blood. The process of how they developed into this fighting force is a fascinating journey to discover.

Roman mythology contains a plethora of fascinating and complex characters. Just as the Greeks had their pantheon of gods, so the Romans had their own pantheon. Every aspect of society was covered by a specific god. The leader of the pantheon of their gods was known as *Jupiter* or *Jove.* Other notable Roman gods include Minerva, Juno, and Mars. The name "pantheon" is borrowed from the Greek name for a collection of gods in a culture.

The way of the Roman Empire did not last. Due to numerous issues, the empire eventually fell due to poor governance, a weakened military, and outside influence from barbarian invaders. The fall of the Roman Empire in the West led to the Dark and Middle Age periods of which few written records remain.

Roman history is a journey of discovery, and it needs to be approached with an open mind. By doing so, we can begin to unlock the secrets of the empire and what it meant in the context of world history.

CHAPTER 1: TIMELINE

The Three Periods Of Ancient Rome

Roman civilization can be divided into three distinct periods. These periods encompass the complete progression of the empire, from its birth in 700 BC, to its decline and fall in around 600 AD. The names of these periods are disputed amongst historians. According to *The Roman Empire: A Brief History* (n.d), the three periods (apart from the founding itself) are the Period of Kings, Republican Rome, and Imperial Rome.

The Founding of Rome

According to *This Day In History* (n.d) there are two versions of the founding of Rome: one mythological, or legendary, version and one historical account. According to mythology, Rome was founded by Romulus and Remus on the Tiber River in about the 7th century AD. The origin of the exact date of Rome's founding can be attributed to Roman scholar Marcus Terentius Varro in the 1st century.

The Legend

Legend holds that Romulus and Remus were twin sons of the mythical figure Rhea Silvia, the daughter of King Numitor. Silvia and Numitor lived in Alba Longa, a city in the Alban Hills, situated southeast of Rome itself. Numitor was deposed by his younger sibling Amulius. The evil Amulius tried to force Rhea Silvia to become a vestal virgin, thus depriving her of the ability to have sons who could one day challenge him for the throne. However, Mars, the god of war, impregnated Rhea Silvia and she gave birth to twin sons Romulus and Remus. While the villainous King Amulius ordered the babies to be killed by drowning them in the Tiber River, they survived and were later found and suckled by the she-wolf at the foot of Palatine hill. A shepherd, Faustulus, then rescued them, or so the story goes. Faustulus raised the boys until they became hardy and strong. Forming a band of warriors with other men, they attacked Alba Longa and killed Amulius, passing the throne back to their grandfather while establishing a town on the banks of the river where they were discovered. However, things did not end well for the family. Some time later, Romulus and Remus had a disagreement, and Remus was killed in the scuffle. Romulus then took over the settlement on the river and named it after himself, Rome.

How Rome Was Born

As legend suggests, Rome was indeed founded on the banks of the Tiber River in 700 BC. According to Joshua J. Mark (2009), Rome began as a small town that grew in strength and stature. She was ruled by seven kings for a period of about 200 years. Having observed the nearby Greek way of life, the small tribe began to mimic the neighboring society's improvements in culture and architecture. The Roman tribe looked at the stronger Etruscans of the north and noted their lifestyle and technological advances. Etruria was already a well-established settlement and seemed to have a significant impact on the development of the Roman settlement at this time. The positioning of Rome to the river meant that trade could flourish, agriculture growth thrived, and water was readily available. This mirrors how the mighty Egyptian Empire itself had come to be many, many thousands of years earlier - by relying on the strength of the Nile River. As Rome grew stronger, she came into contact with neighboring settlements. From her earliest years, she proved to be great at learning from the tribes around her, and by around 600 BC, she was a thriving and prosperous city. A tiny town no more, the seeds of what would eventually become the mighty kingdom of Rome had already been sown. In around 500 BC, the last of the seven kings of Rome was deposed, namely, Tarquin the Proud. A man named Lucius Junius Brutus then abolished the monarchy and established the very first Roman Republic.

Expansion

Rome had yet to realize the full potential of her military might in the earliest years of the empire, although it was beginning to show signs of branching away from trade and towards a more expansionist mindset. According to Wasson (2016), "the history of the city is mired in stories of valor and war." After the fall of Tarquin the Proud, the last king of Rome, the rest of the 5th century BC was marked by struggle. Many significant events were to shape the growth of the realm. After the fall of the monarchy in 509, little is known about the next 70 years, as few written records survive. The city was starting to become the dominating force on much of the Italian peninsula, but it was not without sacrifice. Other neighboring tribes noted the lack of leadership and control over the city itself, and they sought to besiege it.

According to *Roman Republic (509 BC - 27 BC)* (n.d), many people within the city itself were divided between wanting to return to the monarchy and wanting to remain a republic, which led to conflict within the republic itself. Rome had to contend with neighboring tribes who wanted to put an end to the fledgling state, threatened by her dominance. Notable battles at this point included the Pyrrhic Wars, the battle of Regallus, and conflicts against Greece, the Samnites, and the Etruscans themselves.

The legal system of Ancient Rome was beginning to be established, and the seeds were being sown for what would later become the mightiest empire the world has ever known. In 450 BC, the Law of the Twelve Tables was drafted (in Latin, Lex XII Tabularum). This is amongst the earliest iterations of Roman law, and it laid out how citizens were to be treated, with both fairness and equality. These bronze tablets formed the foundation for future Roman legal doctrine. According to *The Twelve Tables* (n.d), the tablets contained statutes for all kinds of legal situations, from public laws to matters of justice. The codification of these tablets was a sign that Rome was moving towards a more structured form of society, one that would endure through the ages.

The Seeds Of The Empire

By the time 27 BC arrived, Rome was advanced both technologically and in terms of its civilization and society. Rome was ready to become an empire. But, to do so, Romans would need to expand and grow further and further. The republic was in political turmoil and there was unrest in the streets, namely at the battle of Gallia Aquitania, wherein General Agrippa won a great victory over the rebels.

Many felt that Rome was about to fall due to this

unrest created by the civil war between different factions within the republic. The Roman citizenry was falling victim to the corruption and vice that was plaguing the city (Wasson, 2016). A kind of evil was springing up caused by moral decay and reckless living. The event that eventually led to the formation, or transition, from republic to empire was the creation of the triumvirate, an alliance between three major figures in Roman history: Julius Caesar, Crassus, and Pompey, all of whom had agendas for ruling Rome. These three men took power away from the Senate and leveraged it to themselves. Because the Senate had been in charge of Rome when it was a republic, it was previously up to the Senate to decide the direction the government took and to oversee transitions of power, but the triumvirate severely weakened the Senate's role. This newfound dictatorial power gave the new triumvirate political leverage over the plebeians (or, common folk). Over time, one of these men would grow more influential than the others, and would eventually become a dictator over all of Rome. His name, of course, was Julius Caesar, the first of the great political figures in Ancient Rome, and probably the greatest Roman ruler who ever lived. At the time, though, the three men consented to put their differences aside and rule the fragmented Republic. The beginnings of this alliance had been sown many years earlier, however.

Caesar, Pompey, and Crassus
Ten years earlier, a man by the name of Spartacus, a

gladiator from the arena, had led a rebellion through the streets of Southern Italy. The rebels' motivation was simple: they no longer wanted to be slaves. The revolt carried on for so long that the Senate sent Crassus to put down the uprising; however, he did not receive the due credit for doing so because Pompey, returning from Spain, had claimed the glory for crushing the rebellion himself. The two men continued to view each other with distrust, but both were named co-consuls in around 70 BC for their part in that victory over the rebels.

In 67 BC, Rome was facing a food shortage. Rampant piracy had meant that trade routes were being affected, and widespread shortages of precious resources resulted. Pompey was tasked with dealing with these pirates and also a man named Mithridates, ruler of the kingdom of Pontus who kept besieging Roman provinces. After Mithridates was defeated and the pirate threat was similarly extinguished, Rome enjoyed a period of relative calm. However, Pompey's campaigns in the Mediterranean were to fundamentally change the nature of the empire and redraw the map to the east of the empire. By the time he returned in 62 BC, Pompey's vision had changed, and he desired land for his military veterans. This was not to be forthcoming from the Senate, but it did highlight Pompey's agenda: to rule over a territory of his own.

What is clear is that each member of the triumvirate had their reasons for wanting to rule Rome. Pompey hoped for military glory and living space for his soldiers. Caesar wanted to attain the role of "Consul" and therefore a share in the ruling powers of Rome. Crassus desired to benefit financially and economically. Caesar was already a military man, having returned from Spain in triumph. He had something that the others lacked: charisma. However the three men might have felt about each other, they elected to remain as a three-pronged ruling party, keeping power away from the people and the Senate. Caesar succeeded in uniting Crassus and Pompey in an uneasy truce due to their differences of opinion on policy. In 59 BC, Caesar was elected Consul of Rome, one of the most powerful positions in the land, as it was the ruling head of the Senate. In this position, he was able to exert influence over the other two members of the triumvirate. He increased the number of members of the Senate to 900 and began to command the loyalty of the army itself. The Senate, now extremely fearful of Caesar's influence, ordered him to release command of the army, but Caesar refused.

The Rule of Caesar
Although Julius Caesar did not rule for a long time, his impact on the Roman world and the course of history cannot be denied. After his election to Consul, he attempted to consolidate his rule and expand the empire at the same time. One of his notable achievements was the conquest of Gaul in around 58 to 50 BC. Caesar was noted as being an astute and

ruthless general, having been involved in the military all his life while in Spain. However, he had made many enemies during his time in the upper political echelons of Rome. What happened next was to further damage the fragile relationship between the triumvirate: Crassus was killed in the battle of Carrhae in 53 BC. This left the less popular Pompey and the immensely popular Caesar. By this time, Caesar was the sole Consul of Rome, and Pompey lived in Caesar's shadow. It was clear that there was only going to be one ruler of Rome and that Pompey would have to wait.Pompey grew increasingly jealous of Caesar and his increasing influence, and the relationship between the two men soured. Caesar then started a civil war in 49 BC, leading an army across the river Rubicon, going against the wishes of the Senate. In the years that followed, political resistance to Caesar's rule was swiftly extinguished and a period of relative stability followed. Caesar was now the sole dictator of Rome, unchallenged in terms of his power.

The Assassination of Caesar
Julius Caesar's rule did not last long. Despite the reforms that he had brought to Rome and the changes he had wrought in society, a group of his political enemies got together in March of 44 BC and assassinated him. It was a seemingly premature end to one of the world's great rulers. His legacy cannot be overstated. He ended the line of republican rulers, took power away from the Senate, expanded the em-

pire greatly, introduced societal change, and introduced Rome to a new era: the era of the emperors. From this time forward until her eventual decline 400 years later, Rome would always be ruled by an emperor.

The Time Of The Emperors

The Second Triumvirate

After Caesar's death, a new triumvirate was formed. When Caesar died, Marc Antony took over the leadership of the empire, but he still had to deal with Caesar's killers. To placate these men, an arrangement was made between Antony and the plotters of Caesar's downfall, Brutus and Cassius. They were made governors of provinces in the empire, but this angered Caesar's adopted son Octavian, according to *Second Triumvirate* (n.d). After stirring up several disgruntled Roman war veterans against Antony, Octavian attempted to lead a revolt at Modena. After defeating Antony in battle, Octavian returned to Rome and demanded to be made Consul - forming an alliance with none other than Antony himself. Backed up by another influential figure in what was once Caesar's army, Marcus Aemilius Lepidus, the three decided to form the new collective dictatorship of Rome. The three rulers collectively made decisions on behalf of Rome and made reforms to weaken the Senate, provide farmland for Caesar's soldiers, execute a slew of political opponents, and, at Phillipi, defeat the forces responsible for the plot to murder Caesar. Brutus and Cassius killed themselves during the battle.

Battle at Sicily

Enemies of the regime banded together at Sicily under the leadership of the son of Pompey, Sextus. In 36 BC, Sexus was defeated in battle at the battle at sea. This incident also led to the end of the triumvirate, as Lepidus was relieved of his powers after angering Octavian by demanding that Octavian leave Sicily. Half of Lepidus' army defected to Octavian's side, showing his influence. Five years later, Antony and Octavian went to war because Antony had fallen in love with the stunning Ptolemaic queen Cleopatra. Deciding that Antony was divided in his loyalty to the empire, Octavian attacked and defeated Antony with the help of the skilled general Agrippa. Octavian then assumed sole leadership of Rome, united the empire, and was considered one of Rome's greatest leaders until his death in 14 BC. In fact, his reforms lead to Rome becoming as powerful as she would ever be due to one small phrase: Pax Romana.

Pax Romana

With the quelling of the civil unrest, Rome had entered a new phase of world dominance. No more was she to be on the offensive. Rome was beginning to embrace the idea of consolidating its power in the lands that she already owned. The next 200 years were spent in peaceful imperialistic conquest, marked by fewer wars than there had been previously. The empire grew and was strengthened. Although there were a number of revolts, the Roman government was able to quell these incidents and keep the peace. Trade and industry with neighboring countries was enhanced. This period lasted until around 180 AD according to *The Pax Romana* (2021).

After the battle at Sicily, Octavian returned to Rome and set himself up as the sole ruler of the empire. However, he was careful not to flex his authority to the Senate as Julius Caesar had done, according to *The Pax Romana* (2021). He was careful to maintain a balance between his absolute power and the traditional structures of the republican government. The Senate took kindly to Octavian and bestowed the honorary title "Augustus" on him when he attempted to voluntarily give up his powers in 27 BC. The term Augustus means "the majestic one" in Latin. And Augustus certainly was a great ruler deserving of the name. In his 41 years as ruler of Rome, the empire experienced stability as it had not experienced before.

One of the key areas in which Rome became more and more powerful was in the field of technology. The discovery of concrete enabled them to build massively powerful buildings and structures and led to the formation of roads, which at that time were not the most developed part of any region's communication structures. The building of mighty monuments, such as the Pantheon, out of concrete solidified the idea that Roman culture was dominant. Such structures were symbols of the rule of law and order within the empire. Some of the greatest literary minds in world history were born during this period: the likes of Virgil, Ovid, Livy, and Horace. One could say that the Roman way of life became entrenched in society, and, for much of the world, Rome was seen as the bastion of law, order, and civilization in the West. It was impossible to imagine the world without Rome. All was not perfect, however. The empire still had some growing pains. Not all emperors could be trusted.

Caligula
For example, one of the great tragedies in Roman history came after the death of Augustus in 14 AD. The emperor that came after him was the evil Caligula, a sadistic man who took pleasure in the sufferings of others. He was so awful that the Senate turned against him and had him executed in 41 AD by his own Praetorian guard.

Christianity In Ancient Rome

It is important to be aware of the social and political issues that Rome faced during her rise, development, and eventual decline as a world power. In an empire where loyalty to Caesar was seen as the highest honor a civilian could give, personal and religious views were sometimes seen as threats because they challenged the assumptions that Rome was built on - the notion that Caesar was a god and that Rome was all-powerful. Nowhere is this more clearly demonstrated than in the instance of the rise of Christianity as a popular belief system. When the personal beliefs of citizens collided with their duty to Rome, there was often conflict between them. Founded by Jesus Christ and later expanded on by the Apostle Paul, the message of Christianity started spreading at around 40 AD. Despite attempts by the government to control it, the message continued to grow even to the furthest corners of the empire. This naturally caused a huge divide amongst the Christians of Rome (this was the name that the scornful Romans had given those who believed in the teachings of Christ), and the people who worshipped the local Roman deities. According to *Rome And Christianity* (2015), those who followed Christianity were frequently the poor and slaves. They were often badly treated and in 64 AD, the evil emperor of the time, Nero, blamed the Christians for setting the great fire which destroyed much of the Circus Maximus. From this moment on, Christians were even more persecuted than they had been, and they were executed at every opportunity. This persecution led to what must have been a common practice for people fearing for their lives and safety during that time: Christians decided to operate underground in the catacombs and waterways under Rome where their activities would not be discovered. This persecution of Christians would continue until the Emperor Constantine removed the restriction on practicing religion in 313 AD.

The Five Good Emperors

Not all Roman emperors were morally corrupt. What largely contributed to the stability of the Pax Romana was the succession of wise and stoic Roman emperors after the death of Caligula. These emperors were: Nerva, Trajan, Hadrian, Antoninius Pius, and Marcus Aurelius, the final upright emperor of the Pax Romana. According to *Five Good Emperors* (n.d), there were small signs of weakness in the empire at this point, but they went largely unnoticed for many, many years. The evil Emperor Commodus, however, put an end to this era of Roman peace. Troubled times were to follow. In the early part of the 2nd century, however, things seemed to be going well. Rome was at the peak of her powers under the great Emperor Trajan. Her empire stretched to the fullest extent that it could, from Scotland in the north and west, to Babylonia in the east. This was in the year 117 AD.

End of the Pax Romana

In 180 AD, Marcus Aurelius died, leading to a succession of civil wars within the empire that only ended with the death of the evil Commodus in 193 AD. Much damage had been done to the empire at this point. Septimius Severus was the new ruler of Rome and inherited an empire burdened by strife and division. He entered the Senate in 173 AD, and became consul in 190 AD, after a turbulent number of years in the empire. He was the son of an equestrian and was from the Roman colony of Leptis Magna, an ancient Libyan City. The reign of Severus (from around 193 AD to 211 AD) was marked by his constant military campaigns and control over his political rivals. Severus is noted for his favorable treatment of soldiers and veterans and his improvement of their lives. They were given land and special favors and were even allowed to marry while in military service.

During Serverus' time as emperor, it was also notable that he "orientalized" the Roman monarchy, to an extent. This is seen in his priorities, such as establishing more outposts on the Eastern frontier and re-establishing the province of Mesopotamia when he overthrew the Parthians in battle at Ctesiphon. Serverus also oversaw the repair of the Pantheon after it was damaged during the civil war which took place until 197. In 211 AD, Severus died while he was in Britain. For the last few years of his life, he had been battling against the Caledonians there. According to an article entitled "Lucius Severus Septimius" (n.d), there was a rumor that Severus advised his sons to favor the military and army veterans while he was on his deathbed. How true this admonition is, though, is uncertain. What is known, however, is that Rome was entering a newer and more uncertain era. The Severan dynasty following the disastrous era of Commodus is considered to be the beginning of the end of Rome's golden age. The empire would still exist for many hundreds of years, but the tranquility and stability which had been present for so long was now at an end.

The Third Century

The third century in Roman history was a period from 201 AD to around 300 AD. It was a period marked by the beginnings of chronic political instability, economic depression, and major divisions within the empire. Rome was still the major world force, but it was starting to reach the limits of its power. Barbarian tribes from the north and other regions were starting to sense weakness, and much of the 3rd century was marred by fighting. The reign of Aurelian from 270-275 AD brought some measure of stability for a time, but overall, this was a turbulent period in Roman history.

Emperor Diocletian further divided the empire during his period of rule in around 280 AD. Each part of the empire was controlled by a separate ruler called a tetrarch. The Tetrarchy, however, did not survive for very long due to Diocletian's sudden resignation due to illness. He retired peacefully to his vegetable garden in Dalmatia and there lived out the rest of his days. However, trouble was brewing. Diocletian's withdrawal once again threw the empire into chaos.

The slight period of calm that Aurelian had brought was soon forgotten as fresh divisions, factions, and political unrest started to emerge once more.

East and West
In the great city of Naissus in 272 AD, the legendary Constantine was born. Raised under the leadership of Flavius Constantius, one of the leaders of the infamous Tetrarchy, he soon established himself as a divisive figure due to his political and religious leanings. His Greek mother, Helena, was not well-educated or well-known, but Constantine himself was to become one of the great rulers of the struggling Roman Empire, and his time as ruler from 308 to 337 AD was significant for many reasons. Rome was now a fragmented empire and had been so since the rule of Diocletian some years earlier. Constantine managed to unite the factions within the empire once again, although Rome would always now be divided between East and West. By 324, things were once again returning to normal in the Roman Empire, and stability and peace were prevailing. However, the great city of Rome itself was no longer seen as the jewel in the crown. Constantine turned his gaze eastward. Sensing that in the coming years there would be barbarian invasions that Rome would not be able to deal with, Constantine founded the great city of Constantinople in the eastern part of the empire. Constantinople was a much more easily defensible position than the exposed Roman coastline in Italy. Constantinople was to become a

mighty fortress in the years to come, a symbol that Roman strength would always be there, even if it was entrenched in the east and not the west.

The First Christian Emperor

Constantine was unique in that he was the first emperor to embrace Christianity, which up until that point, had been seen as a challenge to the traditional Roman values of worshipping Caesar, the State, and the Roman pantheon. Constantine, on the other hand, did not see things the same way. In 313, he introduced the Edict of Milan, a document that afforded Christians freedom from persecution and freedom to practice their belief system anywhere that they wanted to. This action on the part of the emperor marked a sharp change from what had existed before. Without the fear of death hanging over them, many Christians became even bolder and more active in sharing their faith and beliefs with others.

This did not, however, mean that Christians were more popular amongst the civilian population. The vast majority of Roman citizens still believed in their traditional gods. There were still clear divisions amongst those who believed in the glory of the empire and those who did not. This division between Christian Rome and Pagan Rome would last until the fall of Paganism in around 230 AD.

The 4Th Century And The Decline And Fall Of The Empire

The 4th century marked the beginning of the end for Rome as a world power. This decline had been many years in the making, but when it did happen, it was a swift process. Constantine the Great, the ruler of the western half of the Roman Empire, was content to let others take rulership of the eastern half. In 316 AD, eastern Emperor Licinius who had been sharing power with another Roman ruler, Maximinus, took sole ownership of the eastern half of the Roman Empire. In 324 AD, Constantine fought and defeated Licinius and to reunite the empire once again. This action led to the founding of the city of Constantinople (formerly known as Byzantium). The dedication of the city in 330 AD marked the official division of the Roman Empire for the first time in its history. It was known as the "Second Rome" (Nicol, n.d).

Constantine died in 337 AD after falling ill in Persia. His legacy is found in his Christianization of the Roman Empire and his reforms that established religious freedom rather than in any kind of major legislative overhauls. Constantine's inclusion of Christianity amongst the religions of Rome formed a new cultural outlook in which the Pagan gods of Rome were worshipped alongside the new Christian God. His establishment of the Nicene Creed in 325 AD led to the belief in Jesus as a divine being and is still adhered to this day. His reforms led to the emergence of a new Rome as a Christian state. Politically, he left three sons to carry on his dynasty.

After Constantine, few rulers wanted to take on the challenge of ruling the entire empire alone. It was too vast and too easily attacked by the increasingly emboldened barbarian tribes. Both the eastern and western empires were now coming under increasing pressure from these invaders. According to *Byzantium: The New Rome* (n.d), Italy was invaded by the Ostrogoths, Spain was invaded by the Visigoths, the provinces of North Africa fell to the Vandals, and Gaul fell to the Franks, all at different times during the 4th century.

One of the last rulers to attempt to unite the empire was Theodosius (379 to 395). His ban on Pagan religion helped to entrench the ideals of Christianity within Roman society at that time. When he died, Theodosius bequeathed the empire to his two sons: Honorius in the western half of the Roman Empire and Arcadius in the east.

Because of its more entrenched urban structure and culture, and its more easily defensible position, the eastern Roman Empire fared better in the 3rd and 4th centuries. They were able to use their considerable resources to buy time from the invaders and to placate them with gifts of useless land on the borders of the empire. They hoped that over time, the barbarians would eventually become like the

Romans themselves, naturalized citizens. This tactic seemed to be working for a time. But some barbarian rulers were not satisfied with meaningless trinkets of land. They wanted Rome herself.

The Invasion of the Huns
One of the Romans' principal foes during this period was a particularly dangerous foe known as the Hunnic tribe. Led by a great warlord calling himself Attila the Hun, they ransacked and pillaged much of what remained of the western Roman Empire and continuously threatened the eastern Roman Empire. While he was emperor, Theodosius had attempted to bribe the Huns with the aforementioned useless trinkets of land. The Huns continued to ask for tribute, however. After Theodosius' death, the new Emperor Marcian refused to pay the Hunnic tribute. However, by this time, the barbarian king had focused his attention on what was going on in the west. In 453 AD, Attila died and much of the Hunnic Empire collapsed, leading to fighting amongst various factions in the tribe.

The Decline, Invasion, And Fall Of Rome

What happened in the 5th century was to shape the future of the world for hundreds of years to come. In 476 AD, the western Roman Empire ceased to exist, crushed beneath the weight of ceaseless invasions and sackings. Weakened by economic turmoil, economic hardship, and fragmented military presence, Rome was unable to cope any longer. Odoacer, a Germanic leader, deposed the final Roman ruler of the western Empire, ironically entitled Romulus. It had begun with Romulus, and now it was ending with Romulus. The thousand-year reign of order that the western empire had brought to the world was over.

Life After the Empire

The western Roman Empire was divided up amongst the barbarian tribes. T*he Fall Of The Roman Empire* (n.d) states that waves of barbarians feasted upon the remains of the dying empire. Vandals, Visigoths, Angles, Saxons, Gauls, Lombards, Ostrogoths, and many others took their turn at claiming Roman land. The Angles and the Saxons took over the previously held British Isles, and the Gauls invaded Gaul, or what is today known as France.

CHAPTER 2: THE GEOGRAPHY OF ROME

Rome's Place In The World

Rome was located in the middle of several different countries. It was bordered by Switzerland and Austria to the north, France and the Tyrrhenian ocean to the west, the Mediterranean sea, Greece and the Aegean to the southeast, and Slovenia and the Adriatic to the east. Rome was open to many kinds of trade during times of peace, but it was also vulnerable during times of war because of its exposed coastline.

The Boundaries and Divisions of Rome

Ancient Italy was divided into 3 parts: northern, central, and southern. The northern part of Italy was considered to run from the Alps to the River Macra in the west, to the Rubicon in the east. Southern Italy completed the rest of the "boot" of Rome, comprising four different countries: Lucania and Bruttium in the west, and Apulia and Calabria to the east. Central Italy made up the part of the northern peninsula which was between the Rubicon and the Macra. It comprised the territories belonging to the Samnites, the Etrurians, Campania, and what was known as the Sabellian country.

The Geography of the City

The Location Of Rome

The city of Rome was located around the center of Italy on the banks of the Tiber River. Surrounded by hills, the city of Rome was the hub of communication, trade, industry, and culture during the time of the Roman Empire. Roman roads gave easy access to the city and the surrounding areas, facilitating this trade. Rome was located near many shallower rivers that were not difficult to traverse. However, because Rome was not situated on the coastline itself, it did not have as developed of a navy as other more advanced naval civilizations such as the Greeks. Early Rome was vulnerable to attacks when they were in the water because of these perceived weaknesses.

Geographical Features That Allowed Rome to Thrive

The fact that Rome was far inland was also a strength, because it meant that Rome could not be attacked from the sea. The fact that the Tiber River was present was hugely influential in Rome's rise.

According to *The Geography Of Rome* (n.d), the river provided easy transportation and had many acres of land available for farming, although it was prone to flooding and was also quite marshy. This allowed the agricultural sector of Rome to flourish in its early years. The Alps and Apennines Mountains offered some protection for the empire and were of strategic value when enemies tried to attack the city.

Rome's central location allowed them to exercise strategic trade initiatives with the Greek and Phoenicians. Trading with these nations helped to keep Rome afloat during her formative years and long after them as well. Rome looked at what the surrounding nations around her were doing and copied them. From the Phoenicians, they learned how to ship-build and manage their navy more effectively. Rome's strength lay in their ability to adapt and modify the technologies of the countries around them, and to improve on them. As the Romans found themselves increasingly in need of contact with the sea, they built a harbor at Ostia. During the day, wheeled vehicles were not allowed inside the city of Rome due to the large pedestrian presence there, but by nightfall, carts and wagons poured in from Ostia carrying goods and precious resources.

The Role of the Environment in the Early Development of Rome

In her early years, Rome was primarily a farming and fishing community. This was because of her distance to the river and the fact that large amounts of farmland surrounded the city on the seven hills themselves. This proximity to important natural resources enabled the city of Rome to develop quickly. It was the perfect base from which to begin imperialist conquests later. Once Rome was established on the peninsula, she had all the resources she needed and she was in the perfect position to capitalize on these resources. Being a farming community, grazing was readily available on the hills. Fish were available in the rivers for people to eat. Finally, the hills around the city offered natural protection from any enemies who wanted to attack Rome.

Rome's climate was perfectly suited to agriculture, being that it was mild and temperate. Rome had hot summers and moderate winters which meant that the risk of frost on crops was lessened. They did not experience the severe weather patterns of other nations. The soil in the region of the Tiber River valley was flat, but it was also fertile, allowing for easy distribution and raising of crops and livestock. The plains that were especially beneficial were found in the Po river valley and Campania according to *Geography Of Ancient Rome And Italy* (n.d). A burgeoning population also meant that Rome had a workforce with which to start building its city. Some of these workers were slaves from the local populace and surrounding areas. Central Italy did experience rare snowfall, but it is not known whether the Romans experienced any significant hardship as a result. For the most part, the Roman climate was stable and ideal for an agrarian economy.

The Mountains Of Rome
Rome was built on seven hills. The names of these hills were: Aventine, Palatine, Caelian, Esquiline, Quirinal, Viminal, and Capitoline. It is also worth noting that Italy itself was 80 percent mountainous according to *Geography of Ancient Rome And Italy* (n.d). There was an extraordinarily varied amount of mountainous and hilly terrain in Rome, all of which offered defensive tactical advantage, or stone for masonry that was used in the construction of buildings for many hundreds of years.

Some of the mountains bordering Rome include the Apennines, the Alps, the Matterhorn, Mt. Blanc, the Dolomites, and many others. Rome was also home to two of the world's most well-known and fierce volcanoes: Mt. Vesuvius and Mt. Etna. Vesuvius is of course infamous for being the volcano that buried an entire city, namely Pompeii, and it is still very ferocious to this day. The Romans were noted for making use of the softer volcanic rock in their buildings and constructions as well. Here, it is important to know exactly what the Romans did with the volcanic material that they gathered. Concrete was one of the great secrets of the Roman Empire and, to this day, it is still considered one of the great advancements of the ancient world. The Romans used to mix volcanic ash and lime fragments to bind rock fragments together to form a kind of self-healing material. Roman concrete was able to repair itself, to an extent, through the process of crystallization. This substance was impacted by the saltwater of the ocean which changed the structure via chemical reaction, rendering it impenetrable to most ancient devices that could attack it. It is a marvel of ancient engineering. Scientists are still poring over exactly what made Roman concrete such an amazing tool back in the day. All this aside, it was the proximity of these volcanic beasts that enabled Rome to take advantage of their materials. Rome was extremely adept at making the most of the environment they found themselves in.

The Strategic Advantage of Topography
Rome's defensive strength lay in the fact that she could not be easily attacked due to the hilly and mountainous terrain that lay on all sides of her. As an example, one needs to look no further than the battle of Hannibal. In 219 BC, Hannibal of Carthage attempted to overthrow the Roman ally of Saguntum which led to a predictable aggressive response from the Romans.

These conflicts began what is known as the Second Punic War. Hannibal led a massive army through the rocky terrain and into central Italy. Fighting against the shrewd and dangerous Roman general Publius Cornelius Scipio, Hannibal did not find the mountain crossing easy, and lost many of his troops to the climate and the harsh terrain. Hannibal eventually prevailed against Scipio but was later defeated; the challenge of overcoming the Roman army in their own lair was too great. This exemplified the fact that crossing the mountains with an army of any size was a large undertaking for even the most skilled of commanders. The hilly terrain Rome was faced with saved her on numerous accounts in battle. During her early years, it likely saved her from being overwhelmed by the larger and much more powerful tribes that surrounded her such as the Samnites, Etruscans, and Greeks.

Roman Roads

The geography of Ancient Rome enabled her to more effectively trade with the nations around her. As Rome became more sophisticated, roads were developed. The purpose of these roads was to facilitate movement in and out of the city daily. Troops could be maneuvered more quickly in a hurry, food supplies could be easily shifted, and people themselves could more effectively move around the city. Rome's central position meant that her roads could be connected to ports and other cities more efficiently. Rome was ahead of the curve in this regard. Because of the development of these roads, the empire was able to expand and develop at a faster pace. Men and materials could be transported more easily, and the furthest reaches of the empire could be patrolled and garrisoned more regularly. Rome grew culturally and economically stronger due to the improved systems of communications between the provinces. A journey on horseback might have taken several weeks to tramp across rough terrain. With the aid of a road, it became a much more streamlined process.

Types of Roads

Roman roads were divided up into three specific categories. There were the *via publica (via munita), via vicinalis,* and *via privata.* The *via publica* were the public roads, as the name suggests. They were used for wheeled, mounted, and pedestrian traffic and could be thoroughfares, but they could also be cul-de-sacs (*diverticulum*) ("Via Publica," 2019). The other term used was *via munita,* but over time, this came to mean the same thing. The *via vicinalis* were roads designed for general use within the provinces and sometimes running across private land. *Via privata* were small roads constructed without the aid of the government that ran across an individual's property, and they were also known as country roads. The public could still access these roads if they needed to. The *Via Militaris* was a specific road used by military units and troops that ran across the northern border of the empire along the length of Danube. It was of vital importance because of the need to funnel troops to this far-off area quickly if the situation demanded it. A road in this part of the empire made the process of transporting troops, supplies, and equipment a lot more efficient.

Roman roads had specific names if they were used for a particular purpose or had cultural and historical significance. One of the most famous roads in all of Rome was the *Via Appia* or, *Appian Way*, as it is known in English. It was one of the first Roman roads to be constructed in around 312 BC, and its length was about 560 km. It led to the development of further roads, and at the height of the empire's power, almost 80,000 km of roads had been developed. According to *The Roman Empire, c125 CE* (n.d), the Romans also built the world's first dual carriageway which was named *Via Portuensis.* It connected the Roman harbor at Ostia to the city itself and made transporting precious materials, cargo, and supplies much easier. At the center of Rome itself was a monument known as the *milliareum aureum* or the "golden milestone." It was said to be the central point from which all Roman roads originated. When the western Roman Empire collapsed, the system and network of roads collapsed along with it. The Roman network of roads and transportation systems is an indicator of how they approached life. Their ways of construction were just another sign of the manner in which the empire was organized, which in turn led to their success through the ages.

Management of Roads

Roman roads were set up for efficiency. Traveling speed was enhanced by placing stables every 15 km or so along the routes with fresh horses should travelers need them. Refreshment stations existed along these routes for the benefit of weary travelers and those traveling with their families. It was estimated that the average traveler could manage about 40 km in a day and thus the stations were set up at these intervals. However, this was not a hard and fast rule. Many travelers and courier services could travel further distances if they needed to. Many people preferred to travel longer distances via ships, as they were less taxing, although they were also more expensive. Overall, roads were an important part of the geography of Rome because they showed how Romans overcame the terrain and obstacles that they were faced with, turning the land into an advantage while expanding the empire.

CHAPTER 3: THE MAIN FIGURES IN ROMAN HISTORY

Political Figures

Emperors

The very first thing people think of when they hear the term 'Ancient Rome' are the leaders, both good and bad, of this great nation. After she became a monarchical dictatorship, leaving behind the ideas of state and Senate, these men determined the fate of Rome. It is worth noting that every ruler of the Roman Empire had something about them that was unique to that particular ruler.

The greatest of these leaders was the mighty Julius Caesar. He was a renowned military man, a charismatic speaker, and a great leader of men. Born in 100 BC, he rose to power and through the ranks as a Roman general. He took on the governorship of Hispania in 61 BC. After his pact with Pompey and Crassus in 59 BC, Julius Caesar assumed the role of Consul of Rome. His next eight years were spent in conquest of Gaul and he eventually assumed the role of absolute authority in the Roman hierarchy. Julius Caesar was also a very complex character and one who has been analyzed throughout history. His intelligence and craftiness helped him to gain the edge in tactical and military situations. He was an expert strategist and was able to get out of seemingly disadvantageous situations using his amazing powers of negotiation. One such example of this is when he found himself captured by pirates while on his ocean travels. According to *Julius Caesar* (2019), he convinced his captors to raise his own ransom and then organized a naval force to attack and kill them.

Julius Caesar's status rose even further when he attacked and defeated Mithridates IV of Pontus who had laid siege to several Roman cities. Soon after these military conquests, he cunningly arranged an agreement with two other powerful Roman allies which allowed him to maintain a foothold in power, where he stayed until he could eventually assume total control of Rome.

The reign of Caesar came to a premature end in 44 BC. His mistake was trusting others with his life. He allowed the wrong types of people into his circle: Brutus and Cassius. While Caesar might have known that his life was in danger, he was unable to determine who wanted to kill him. He was betrayed by those he trusted, and this trust was, in the end, a fatal character flaw.

The assassination of Caesar during the Ides of March is considered to be one of the landmark events in Ancient Roman history. It cemented what was already a firm transition to the new era of the emperors and marked further movement away from the idea of a republic.

Furthemore, one great Roman Emperor (and some might say the greatest) was the man known as Octavian, or otherwise known as Caesar Augustus. Augustus was the term given to him by the Senate as a way of honoring him. During his time in power, Augustus treated the Senate fairly and made sure to never promote himself, like Julius Caesar had. One senses this was a wise decision as it seemed to make him a popular figure.

In the article "8 things you may not know about Augustus" (2018), we learn that he was born in 63 BC, around the time that his adoptive father Julius Caesar was preparing to take full ownership of Rome. He is considered the very first emperor of Rome.

Augustus lived in more modest quarters than other Roman emperors. He refused to refer to himself as a monarch and appeared more reasonable and humble than many other Roman rulers. His power, however, was greater than any other ruler before him.

A noted tactician, Augustus was able to expand Rome's borders greatly. As a teenager, he went to war against Mark Antony and defeated him, and later expanded the Roman influence north into Germania across the Rhine, and also south into Egypt and North Africa. However, Augustus did suffer some major defeats. In 9 AD, three divisions of Roman legions were destroyed when they were attacked by barbarian tribes across the Rhine. Augustus was so broken that he banged his head against the wall and cried "give me back my legions," a now-famous line quoted in many works of literature.

Another great and interesting Roman emperor was Antoninius Pius (86 AD to 161 AD). He was unique in his way of ruling Rome because he did not leave the country once. He promoted arts, music, books, culture, museums, science, and the glory of Rome, and there are also no records of any sign of military campaign or war during his reign. This also made him one of the only Roman emperors to not engage in conflict with the surrounding nations. Antoninius Pius rewarded those who practiced the arts and honored those who taught rhetoric and philosophy. He was also involved in the construction of several temples, mausoleums, statues, and theatres. In Roman times, theatres were somewhat different from how we experience them today. They were large, open stone structures where the seating was arranged in a circle, and the performance would take place in the center of the ring.

Hadrian was another very interesting character within the Roman dynasty. Fascinated with the culture of Greece, he attempted to bring some of their ideas to the Roman world. Even though he was never technically given the status of "heir to the throne" by his predecessor Trajan, his wife declared that he was the emperor of Rome not long before Trajan died. Hadrian's rule was marked by his building of the wall, a defensive fortification on the northern borders of the empire. It is marked as the furthest point north that Rome managed to expand. These fortifications still exist to this day and are considered to be one of the landmarks that noted where the borders of the Roman Empire once lay. Hadrian also rebuilt the Pantheon and constructed the temple of Venus and Roma. Overall, he is noted for his more humble personage which is evidenced by reports that he used to camp out with the soldiers after dark instead of lying in state in his luxurious palace.

Marcus Aurelius might be one of the most tragic figures out of the line of Roman Emperors. His rule was a difficult one, coming in during a period of instability and civil unrest. He battled the Parthians in the east, defeated the Marcomanni, Quadi, and Sarmatians in the Marcomannic wars, and generally did his best to try and stave off civil war for as long as possible. Marcus Aurelius was a serious man and was partial to philosophy and pursuing ancient wisdom. What was unique about him could be said to be his desire to write. His book "Meditations" is still published and read to this day. It was written while he was on campaign between 170-180 AD and describes the nature of service to Rome, duty, and maintaining one's dignity even amid hardship and turmoil. After his death, his nickname stuck with him, "The Philosopher."

The next interesting character, Emperor Trajan, presided over what was the height of Roman world dominance. Under him, Rome reached its peak. His reputation as a governor of Rome still endures to this day. Trajan's reforms, actions, and words were all respected by opponents, the Senate, the people, and the army. He was one of the most universally popular rulers in Roman history and with good reason. His rule was philanthropic, and he sought to create a peaceable system of imperialist expansion rather than conquering through all-out war. After Trajan died, Rome never again reached the heights of dominance that it once did. His reign was the zenith of Rome's world rule.

Other emperors were interesting but not for popularity or fame. They got their reputation of violence and lawlessness from their inability to think and rule. One of these awful rulers was the villainous Commodus, who ruled after Marcus Aurelius until he was assassinated in 193. His lust for power and popularity was insatiable. Commodus could not follow in the footsteps of his wise father. Instead, he destroyed his legacy in a few bloody years in the throne that left Rome reeling. His decisions led to the destruction of Roman currency and the weakening of the empire which had taken others before him so long to build. Dio Cassius, a Roman scribe wrote that Commodus turned Rome from a kingdom of gold to one of rust. Much of the administrative work of running the empire was left to servants and co-rulers. Commodus preferred to spend his time watching and organizing the Roman games where he would hunt and kill animals for sport. He would also fight in the arena itself, although the men he fought were often handicapped themselves, making his victory inevitable. Eventually, his colleagues grew tired of his rule and he was assassinated while he was in the bath in 193 AD.

Famous Writers

Roman writers were a diverse and interesting crowd. Spanning hundreds of years, their works continue to be relevant even to this day. Roman writers covered a vast range of subjects including their own versions of the history of the empire, politics, religion, philosophy, science, the natural world, culture and poetry, and many more topics. Roman poets belong to their own specific special grouping, as their form of literature is unique and fascinating. Roman poetry incorporates the mythology and lore of the time. As the periods shifted and seasons changed, the focus of these writers' work also altered. The subject matter tells us what was influential during these periods.

Some 1st Century Roman Writers

Valerius Maximus was a writer that lived during the time of the Emperor Tiberius. His work dealt with famous deeds, battles, and the achievements of Rome. His work seemed to be primarily focused on the realities of Rome rather than fictional constructions.

Aelius Saturninus was another Roman writer living in the first century who was noted for having written some scurrilous documents about the Emperor Tiberius. His punishment was to be thrown from the Tarpeian Rock.

Scribonius Largus was a medical writer who lived under the reign of Emperor Claudius. His works are interesting primarily because they highlight the Roman approach to medical science at this early point in history. His work *De Compositione Medicamentorum Liber* is a long list of medical compositions dealing with medical recipes, herbs, and remedies.

Lucius Junius Moderatus Columella was a former soldier turned farmer. His works deal with agriculture, plants, and different kinds of trees which were common to the region and further afield in the empire. He wrote about this in *De Re Rustica* and *De Arborius.*

Publius Cornelius Tacitus is considered by many to be one of the greatest, if not the greatest, Roman writers and historians. Born in 56 AD, he became a notable Roman orator and public speaker.

But it was his written work that caused the biggest stir. Amongst Publius Cornelius Tacitus' works, *Germania*, *Historiae,* and *Annals* are widely regarded as some of the finest specimens of Ancient Roman literature dealing with a wide range of topics from Roman politics to popular subjects of the time. However, it is his work written about Jesus Christ that is still his most valuable writing. Although much of what was written was lost, some fragments remain. Within the text *Annals* there is a specific reference to Christ and his followers ("Tacitus on Christ," n.d). Tacitus tells of a man named *Christus* who was executed under the orders of Pontius Pilate. His teachings, however, continued to cause division and unrest within the Roman capital.

This source highlights the fact that there was a man named Christus or Christ and that his followers were being persecuted during the time of the Emperor Nero who blamed them for the Great Fire in 64 AD. Extra-Biblical texts like this are incredibly valuable to Christian scholars, those who study the scriptures, and Biblical archaeologists.

The works of Tacitus are also noted for their commentary on Roman society at the time. His histories cover the times of Nerva, Trajan, Nero, Tiberius, and Caligula. Much of his work has been lost in the mists of time, however.

Plinius Maior, known as Gaius Plinius Secundus, or more popularly known by the name Pliny the Elder, was a writer, philosopher, and commander of the

Roman fleet. His most famous work is the *Naturalis Historia*, a work dealing with all kinds of subjects relating to natural history such as mining, astronomy, botany, farming, and art.

Some 2nd Century Roman Writers
Quintus Septimus Florens Tertullianus, better known by his common name Tertullian, was a well-known Roman Christian writer from the 2nd century. His works of theology are still popular even to this day. It was his work *Apologeticus* that led to the modern Christian discipline of Apologetics, or the defense of the Christian faith by upholding its values and precepts.

Vibia Perpetua was a Carthaginian writer and noblewoman who was captured and imprisoned in Carthage during the reign of Severus in around 200 AD. She was both a Christian and a slave, and she kept a diary of her experiences called *Passio Sanctarum Perpetuae et Felicitatis,* or The Passion of the Saints. She was martyred on the emperor's birthday in 203 AD.

Pliny the Younger was another well-respected Roman author from the second century who was the adopted son of Pliny the Elder. He was a lawyer and an administrator in Rome who wrote a series of letters to friends and colleagues which would later become noteworthy. As he rose through the ranks of Roman society to eventually become Consul, Pliny the Younger gained much exposure to the ways of Roman politics and also everyday life. His viewpoints on life at the top echelons of Roman society have become critical to our understanding of the reasons why the Romans thought and acted the way that they did during this time period. Pliny the Younger's relationship with the Emperor Trajan and also with Tacitus himself were significant because they gave him insight into the workings of both the common man and those at the very top of the hierarchy. Some of the contents of his letters detail the eruption of Mt. Vesuvius, other letters are addressed to Trajan asking for advice on what to do regarding the policies relating to Christianity, a rising new belief system at the time. His letters were also known as *Epistulae* in Latin.

One of the greatest Roman minds of the 2nd century was a man by the name of Marcus Tullius Cicero, or simply Cicero for short. According to *Cicero (106-43 B.C.E)* (n.d), he was a gifted orator and speaker, and perhaps one of the most influential figures of the first century behind Julius Caesar himself. Cicero's death coincided with the fall of the Roman republic, and he was there to witness its transition into the era of the emperors. His writings always placed value on political matters over those of the philosophical, and given his station as a lawyer and orator, this is hardly surprising. Although much can be said about the life, thought, writings, ideas, and activities of Cicero, the most significant aspects of his life was his influence on future philosophers such as Augustine.

Some 3rd Century Roman Writers

Apicius is most likely brought up when referring to Ancient Roman cuisine, as his works deal with recipes and dishes of the time. When he was born is not entirely certain, but he is most well-known for his work *De Re Coquinaria*. However, there is confusion over the exact ownership of this work. It is ascribed to Apicius because of the heading on one of the two remaining manuscripts which reads API CAE. According to "List of Roman Authors" (n.d), some of the recipes may be attributed to Apicius and but not exactly written by him. There may have been several people called by this name, and no one is quite sure of the origins of the book. It is known, however, that many Roman celebrities liked to put their names to specific recipes as a mark of honoring themselves.

Pontius of Carthage, also known as Pontius the Deacon, was a deacon serving in the employ of St. Cyprian (Cyprianus). After Cyprianus was arrested and martyred, Pontius wrote *Vita Cypriani*, a work on the life and times of Cyprianus.

Novatian was a religious figure and writer during the rule of Emperor Elagabalus (Heliogabalus). He was a controversial figure in the Catholic Church because he was an antipope (someone who attempts to usurp the Pope despite the office already being filled). He wrote extensively on restrictions within the Biblical Old Testament, public games, and the importance of remaining chaste and pure.

Some 4th Century Roman Writers

In the years after Constantine the Great, many Roman writers turned to Christianity, and this is evident through many of the philosophical texts at the time.

Eusebius Sophronius Hieronymus, also known as Hieronymus or St. Jerome, was a secretary or assistant to Pope Damasus the 1st. He is most notable for his work on translating the Hebrew scriptures into Latin. This is known as the Vulgate translation and is held as canon by the Catholic Church to this day. He wrote notes on the Biblical gospels, commentaries, letters and a work containing information on 135 other Christian authors called *De viris illustribus.*

Augustinus, also known as St. Augustine of Hippo, was a philosopher and thinker in the latter part of the empire's years. He was a writer, theologian, and Christian bishop from what is modern-day Algeria. His influence is still felt to this day, and his grace, humility, and wisdom continues to inspire many.

Aurelius Prudentius Clemens was a poet, jurist and writer, and governor from northern Spain. His work *Psychomachia* is a commentary on the spiritual struggle Christians sometimes experience in their daily lives, but he also wrote numerous hymns and songs.

Poets, Artists, And Musicians

Famous Roman Poets

Virgil, Ovid, and Horace are names that often come to mind when people think of the most notable Roman poets. But throughout the history of the empire, we find that the culture of poetry appreciation was flourishing in Roman society from its beginning to end. Many minor names are becoming more appreciated contemporarily as people delve into the depths of Ancient Roman prose and verse.

One of the most famous of the poets, of course, is Virgil who wrote *The Aeneid*, a poem about a Trojan hero named Aeneas. It is also a commentary on the history and reality of Rome up to the point that it was composed.

Horace was another legendary Roman poet who wrote the *Odes, Satires*, and *Epistles.* His style of poetry can be described as lyric poetry.

Ovid's most famous work is known as *Metamorphoses* which details the fictional account of Julius Caesar and his rise to godhood. Ovid is also known for writing numerous love poems.

Roman poets sometimes put their words to music and created compositions and songs. Often, they would create simple notations that other musicians could use to play along with the words of their poems and songs.

Roman Music

Music is as engrained in Roman history and culture as it is in our own modern-day culture and history. Roman music is depicted in literature, art, and on mosaics as using woodwind instruments, pan flutes, small stringed instruments, cane reed instruments, and harps, amongst others. The Romans also made use of percussion and brass. In the desolate ruins of Pompeii, modern-day archaeologists found remains of shell trumpets, bone flutes, and bronze horns ("Music in Ancient Rome," n.d). Little is known of the system of Roman musical notation itself. But, who were the most effective exponents of these musical instruments?

Music was popular amongst the emperors themselves. Roman Emperor Titus (81-79 AD) was greatly interested in music according to Ancient Roman writer Suetonius ("Music in Ancient Rome," n.d). According to Suetonius, Titus played the harp skillfully and used to amuse his secretaries with his fast finger work with shorthand writing.

Hadrian was also fascinated by music and was very proficient at the flute in particular. He was also good at singing according to *Music in Ancient Rome* (n.d).

Nero, the great and evil emperor of the 2nd century, was said to have played the lyre while Rome burned in the Great Fire of 64 AD. While this may or may not be entirely accurate, it seems that he did have a definite interest in music.

As for celebrity musicians in Rome, there doesn't seem to be much material surviving from that period that would suggest certain people were particularly well-known for their performances. However, there is evidence of plays and dramas incorporating music into them. One such example is the famous dramatist Terence. Born in North Africa, he was taken as a slave to Rome by Terentius Lucanus. His stage plays are noted for being models of "pure Latin" according to *Terence* (n.d). What this shows is that Rome is noted for having talented musicians, poets, and orators of all races and creeds. Their diversity is surprising. Anyone could become a playwright or a famous poet in Ancient Rome if they had the skill and the knowledge to do so.

Famous Military Figures

One would be remiss to analyze a list of the Roman characters in history without looking at the military leaders and players in the Roman army. The Roman military is the central conversation in any discussion about Ancient Rome. Their leaders at the time of the empire were some of the most noteworthy in history, and some have been given a god-like status.

Much has been said about Julius Caesar already, but his prowess as a military leader cannot be understated. His conquest of Gaul was no easy feat. He was by no means the only military leader, though.

One of Rome's greatest (and underrated) generals was a man by the name of Nero Claudius Drusus, who showed brilliant promise early in his career. He was the only Roman general who managed to beat back the Germanic tribes living beyond the Rhine. After being elected to the position of Consul, he rode out once again to battle the Germanic tribes on the Rhine but suffered a terrible fall from his horse and never recovered. His loss was a massive blow for Rome.

Agricola was another of the mightiest generals Rome had ever known. He was most known for being the Roman general who conquered the British isles, or Britannia as they were known at the time. Sent by the Emperor Vespasian, he subdued Britain, led his army all the way to the north of Scotland, built 1300 km of roads, and built up to 60 forts across much of the country. Roman dominance over Britain ensured that she was able to establish Roman culture there which would last for many hundreds of years and still holds true even to this day. Agricola also made sorties around the British coastline under instruction to find out whether Britain was part of the mainland or whether it was in fact an island. In many senses, the battle for Britain was an important step in the development of the Roman Empire, as it established their superiority not only as a military force on land, but also on the water. Agricola was a huge part of this evolution.

Scipio Africanus was a Roman general most noted

for his actions in North Africa and at the battle of Zama. His tactical acumen was well-known throughout the empire during a critical time in Roman history. Born in 236 BC, Scipio quickly rose through the ranks of the Roman army. During the Second Punic War against the legendary general Hannibal Barca, he demonstrated his ability to survive during the Roman failures at Cannae and the battles of Trebia and Ticinus. In 211 BC, Scipio's uncle and father were killed during battle, and he became the new leader of the Roman army. In the years that followed, Scipio managed to capture Carthago Nova in Hispania. This became his new base for operations. Scipio is noted for being a humble man, returning a captured slave woman to the chieftain of her tribe. The leader of the tribe was so grateful that he offered to lend Scipio some troops. Scipio then used his reinforced army to fight and defeat Hasdrubal, destroying the Carthaginian cavalry in the process. In 205 BC, Scipio was made consul of Rome. It was at this point that he fought one of the most famous battles in Roman military history: the battle of Zama.

In 202 BC, both Rome and Carthage were vying for control of the Roman peninsula and the territory that Rome had won in North Africa and Europe. After victories on the Iberian peninsula, Scipio arrived at the ancient city Zama (also known as Xama) in Tunis. Hannibal himself was there with about 6,0000 troops and 6,000 cavalry. Scipio had around

3,4000 troops and about 9,000 cavalry. Scipio was supported by Numidian leader Masinissa, who had a specific kind of cavalry trained to counter the fearful Carthiginian war elephants (they had been trained to get used to the smell and therefore did not panic during the heat of battle). While Hannibal instructed his heavy troops to try and punch holes in the Roman lines, Scipio created gaps for the opposition to funnel through and then used these areas as killzones, creating chaos and confusion by having the Roman troops blow trumpets. Having confused, panicked, and disorganized the enemy, Scipio routed the left flank of the Carthaginian army and routed their cavalry along with the famed war elephants. Hannibal's army was then bested in a hand-to-hand battle with the stronger Roman legionaries. Scipio received great acclaim when he returned to Rome, not only for his military conquest but also for his restraint in not completely destroying the city of Carthage. He was honored with the title "Africanus" for his role in the victories in North Africa.

Gnaeus Pompeius Magnus was a Roman general better known by the name "Pompey." While he is known for being one of the leading figures in the early part of the Roman Empire, he was also a respected general, leader, and tactician. Pompey impressed the Roman ruler Sulla and fought campaigns in Sicily, North Africa, and Numidia. After the death of Sulla in 78 BC, Pompey was sent to Hispania where he was tasked with bringing the resolute King Sertorious to heel. After a protracted struggle, Sertorious was eventually assassinated by one of his own men, and Pompey returned to Rome to quell another attack, this time led by Spartacus. Having successfully accomplished his mission by capturing 5000 of Spartacus' men, Pompey then fell out of favor with his other partner in the soon-to-be triumvirate, Crassus, who felt that Pompey was taking an unfair share of the glory for triumphing in the battle. Nonetheless, the two men would go on to form a powerful alliance with Julius Caesar. In 70 BC, Pompey was elected Consul of Rome and joined with Crassus. For the next 10 or so years, they ruled Rome together until Julius Caesar joined the party in around 60 BC. Pompey had further successes in the 50s, but disaster struck when Crassus was killed in battle at Carrhae. Julius Caesar's influence was becoming more and more evident, and in 49 BC, civil war broke out between the two factions. From this point onward, the legend of Pompey seems to be overshadowed by the more illustrious reign of Caesar.

Another notable Roman general was Germanicus Julius Caesar. Born in 15 BC, he quickly established himself as a top Roman general and made great strides into subduing the barbarian tribes around Germania, hence his name "Germanicus" which was given to him as a mark of honor.

Marcus Vipsanius Agrippa was the key military advisor to the great Caesar Augustus, or Octavian as he was sometimes known. He was most notable for naval battles against Sextus Pompey and for the construction of a harbor at Portus Julius. This harbor linked Lake Avernus and Lucrinus Lacus so that Roman ships could be properly defended in the battle with Sextus. He was responsible for repairs to much of Rome after numerous and costly battles, and he took an interest in improving the city itself and creating festivals for the enjoyment of citizens in the city. Overall, he was a skilled commander and a dutiful servant to Rome.

Aetius was one of the last great western Roman Empire generals. He was born in the 5th century and was a young, daring, and skilled military leader whose speciality was dealing with the threat of the barbarians who now harassed the borders of the Roman Empire on every available occasion. He was tasked with repelling the invasion of the Huns in around 451 AD. Aetius mustered a massive Roman force at the Battle of the Catalaunian fields, made alliances with other barbarian chieftains, and successfully managed to stall the Hunnic invasion of the western Roman Empire at the time. It was one of the bloodiest battles in Roman history, and Attila the Hun's army was broken - as were the Romans. However, Aetius retired from active military service soon after, and the Huns returned not long after that. This time Aetius was not available to save the empire.

In the case of each one of these military commanders, they realized their duty to Rome and fulfilled their calling with distinction. That is why they are remembered throughout history as Rome's finest fighting men.

Gladiators

We have all seen images of gladiators in the arena through TV, movies, and books. These men continue to inspire courage in us through their acts of bravery in the arena.

Roman gladiators and gladiatrices were men and women from all walks of life taken as slaves for every part of the empire. Tasked with entertaining the masses, they were the celebrities of the Ancient Roman world. If they survived, they were treated like royalty. For those not so fortunate, severe injury might have been the best thing that they could hope for. Many were maimed or killed in the arena. What follows is a discussion of some of the most well-known names of men who took on the arena and managed to not only survive, but thrive.

Carpophorus
Carpophorus was the kind of gladiator who takes on wild animals or beasts, also known as a *bestiarii*. The men who were responsible for looking after the beasts were also known as *bestiarii*. Often when man and animal met, there was only one winner. The

vicious creatures gave their tired, hungry, and worn out opponents little chance. However, Carpophorus embraced the challenge and became a living legend. Roman writer Martial states that Carpophorus once killed 20 animals at one time and regularly took on bears, lions, and leopards (Bestiarius, n.d). According to *Top 10 Famous Roman Gladiators* (2020), Carpophorus once saw off a rhino with nothing more than a spear. He was one of the most anticipated gladiators to ever set foot in the arena. The Roman people loved to root for a particular class (or type) of gladiator. Many were trained to use specific weapons depending on their skill and body type. Romans liked to see specific kinds of gladiators pitted against each other and would pay large sums of money betting on who was going to win.

Flamma

Flamma was a slave from Syria who was forced to fight in the arena. His real name was Marcus Calpunius, but he was renamed *Flamma* or "flame" for the arena. He was a class of gladiator known as a *secutor* meaning he carried armor, a heavy shield, and a short sword or gladius into the fights. He won 21 fights and lost about four. He was awarded his freedom but elected to stay and fight in the arena. He died at around age 30 in his final battle. Deaths in the arena were common, but they were sometimes avoided if at all possible. These men were celebrities, and their deaths would send the wrong signals to people watching. Training a gladiator was costly and good money was paid for people to see specific gladiators. The loss of a gladiator through death or injury would have hurt the popularity of the arena games.

Gannicus

Gannicus was considered to be one of the most able gladiators of his generation. Originally hailing from the British Isles, he was noted for his incredible speed, athleticism, and agility. He was able to more easily evade his enemy attacks, and this made him a formidable opponent in the arena. His body was covered in tattoos, one of which represented invincibility. The Romans enjoyed watching agile gladiators as they made the games more exciting. Men like Gannicus would have received top billing.

Spiculus

Spiculus is most known for having ties with the evil Emperor Nero. He was both loyal and supportive of Nero even when it seemed all others were deserting Nero at the time. This impressed the villainous emperor and he granted Spiculus his freedom.

Marcus Attilius

Marcus Attilius is an unusual addition to this list because he might be one of the few gladiators to voluntarily sign up to fight in the arena. He was a free born Roman, not a slave. He was regularly able to hold his own against far more skilled and experienced opponents, and this was evident from early on in his gladiatorial career. He also overcame other notoriously difficult opponents such as Raecius Felix (who had won 12 fights in a row) and Hilarus (another gladiator favored by Nero). Attilius fought in the *murmillo* class using a short sword and a longer shield.

Commodus

Commodus was the tyrannical emperor from the latter part of the 2nd century, but he was also noted for his prowess facing gladiators in the arena. However, how skilled he was is difficult to tell because he would often disable or cripple opponents before getting into the arena with them. Opponents would fight with small wooden swords while Commodus had the real thing. He also enjoyed killing animals which drove down his popularity as a result. His style of fighting was considered unfair amongst the Roman public and he was often jeered. The Romans had a great sense of fairness, and Commodus' actions only served to harm his cause even further.

Tetraites

Tetraites was another gladiator in the *murmillo* class who won notoriety by beating a fellow celebrity gladiator Prudes. He was considered to be one of the strongest gladiators of his generation, and his victory against Prudes is immortalized in graffiti discovered in the ruins of Pompeii back in 1817. Tetraites used to enter the arena without a shirt, but wearing a helmet, and carrying a short sword and a rectangular shield. This would have been considered against type, as most gladiators would armor up as much as possible, depending on what kind of fight they were going to undertake.

Priscus and Verus

Priscus was a Celtic gladiator and was both skilled and powerful in the arena. His partner Verus was also one of the most influential gladiators of his generation. The two used to make a headline act for the games, especially on the opening of the Colosseum. The games themselves consisted of mock naval battles, animal fights, and gladiatorial battles. Under the rule of the Emperor Titus (around 81 AD), these spectacles were intended to try and appease the Roman masses before the entertainment began. Priscus and Verus did end up fighting each other, but such was the respect between these two men that they laid down their arms and did not injure or kill each other. This is still noted as a spectacular development in the history of Roman gladiatorial games, and it is recorded as such. Over time, the two men began to be referred to as a collective rather than as individuals. Roman crowds loved to see a spectacle so the more spectacular the bout, the more people would come to watch the games. Two men fighting on a team would have definitely attracted the attention of the crowds in what was usually a single combat sport.

Crixus

Crixus was a gladiator from Gaul, noted for his size and strength. He trained together with Spartacus at the gladiatorial school known as *Lentulus Batiatus.* A large number of the gladiators, about 70 in total, escaped the school due to the harsh training from their *lanista* (or trainer). They formed a factional group, and under the leadership of Spartacus, attempted to overthrow the Roman government. He was killed during the rebellion.

Spartacus

Spartacus was considered to be one of the greatest, if not the greatest, gladiators of all time. He was a Thracian-turned-Roman-soldier, eventually joining the training school at Capua. His biggest legacy is rebelling against Rome in 71 BC and incurring the wrath of Crassus who arrived bringing 5,0000 troops to crush the revolt. He was killed in the battle of Sicily and his followers were executed in large numbers.

What made these men so great was that they were willing to put their lives on the line in order to impress the mob that was the Roman people. Their bravery and their heroism stands out. Not all great Roman gladiators survived, and many were mortally wounded doing what they felt called to do.

CHAPTER 4: ROMAN LIFE

Romans lived very differently than how we do today, and with very good reason. Their customs, tastes, ways of viewing the world, and their political, economic, cultural and military situations were very different to our modern ways. Their ways of living were dictated by economic prosperity (or lack thereof), whether the empire was doing well and was stable, who was in charge in Rome, and many other factors.

Roman Food And Cooking

Roman Food Habits
Romans ate little food during the day and had a large meal in the evenings. Dinner was the main meal of the day, and preparations would begin at around three in the afternoon. It was as much a time for the family to come together as anything else. Romans did try to eat three meals a day, if possible. This could change depending on what the makeup of a day looked like. If they were richer and had many so-

cial events, they may have more meals. If they were poorer and of a lower social status, they might be lucky to eat at all. For the purposes of consistency, most Romans tended to stick to the three meals a day structure with lighter snacks and beverages in between if needed, much the same as we do today. The first meal was called *ientaculum.* Lunch was known as *prandium* and dinner was known as *cena.*

Dinner was an event that the Romans looked forward to each day, as it gave them the opportunity to rest and relax from the hard labors of the day. How long each meal took depended on the status of the meal. If it was an important meal, it could carry on for several hours, intersected by dancing, speeches, singing, and many other activities. Meals for simple folk took only as long as they needed before they had to resume important activities.

Middle and upper-class Romans tended to recline on couches while they ate at more formal events. This was considered the more comfortable way to eat, and there was no such thing as high tables or they were very rare. Romans typically made use of a low table that they all lay around.

For less formal meals, Romans would stand while they ate or sit on high stools (Ancient Rome: Food and drink, n.d).

Romans did not make much use of knives or forks while eating. Typically they used a spoon for lifting food to the mouth. Forks were sometimes used for spearing food on the table and knives were used for cutting food into more manageable portions much as it is today. Romans also ate with their hands a great deal.

Everyday Foods

One of the most common foods in Ancient Rome was of course bread. This was eaten with every meal of the day. Fruits of all kinds were typical. Vegetables, beans, legumes, cheese, honey, and many other kinds of foods were common. For breakfast, fruit with bread was often eaten early on in the day. Dates, honey, and light wheaten cakes could also form part of this meal, depending on the social status of the eater. Certain foods were easier to access if the person or family happened to be wealthy.

Prandium took place at around 11am. It could consist of fish, vegetables, soup, bread, cheese, or cold meat. Leftovers from the previous day's *cena* might also be served alongside the meal.

Cena was held much later on in the day, and it was at this meal that the most exclusive and expensive food was served. If the family had guests, usually the best food would be served to them at this meal. The same was true in the case of celebratory events such as holidays and feast days. The main meal consisted of three different courses: *gustatio* or *promulsis*, *prima mensa*, and *secunda mensa*. *Gustatio* was an appetizer that could consist of light seafood, eggs, fish, cheese, bread, and vegetables. *Prima mensa* was the main course within the primary meal of the day. It could consist of cooked vegetables, sauces, and meats such as pork, chicken, lamb, beef, and wild game amongst others. More wealthy Romans ate more expensive delicacies such as dormice with honey, peacock tongues, and also strange dishes which might seem unappealing to the modern reader. The more wealthy Romans could afford to be more expansive in their tastes and eating habits than the average Roman citizen. The *secunda mensa* was the dessert course, and it could consist of sweet tarts with honey, fruit, nuts or cakes.

Roman Drinks
Wine was drunk with every meal that the Romans ate. It appeared in many different forms and varieties and was often diluted with water in order to make it last. For example, Romans enjoyed a drink made with warmed wine mixed with different kinds of spices. They also liked *mulsum,* a type of wine mixed with honey. Poorer people drank what they could find, either water or cheap beer. Beer was common in Ancient Rome and was enjoyed by all sectors of society. Coffee did not exist within the Roman world and tea was also non-existent, as herbal infused drinks only made their appearance in modern Europe.

Popular Dishes
Romans enjoyed many kinds of sausages, as they could be customized to the taste of the person mak-

ing them. One particular variety that seems to have stood out in history as being a favorite was the Lucianian sausage. Made with cumin, rue, parsley, seasonings, bay berries, garum, fat, and finely ground meat, this sausage was brought to Rome by the soldiers who had served in Luciana. It was thinly rolled and then smoked.

The Romans also loved eggs. One particular dish that was popular was boiled eggs in various kinds of sauces. They were popular as a snack or an appetizer. One recipe has them served alongside a pepper, lovage, and pine nut sauce.

A common Roman condiment was called *garum*. It can be classified as a type of fish sauce, but it was not like the fish sauce we see in stores today. It was made with the entrails of fresh fish, salt, and herbs such as celery, mint, or oregano. It was diluted with olive oil, vinegar, wine, or water to make it spread further ("What is garum," 2019).

Romans were extremely fond of seafood, and this is evident in their love of mussels. One specific dish that catches the attention is made with leek, *passum* or raisin wine, cumin, and wine. The mussels were cleaned and then cooked within the wine itself until tender.

Roman desserts do not get a lot of attention, but one popular dish was called "pear patina." As the name implies, it is a dessert made with ground pears, cumin, honey, *passum, garum*, and olive oil, made into a *patina* (or a small flat dish), combined with eggs and pepper.

Libum was a type of Roman cheesecake made with flour, ricotta cheese, eggs, and honey and scented with bay leaves. Dishes such as this one were often cooked covered using a dish or cover known as a *testo* (Raimer, 2000).

Food for the Rich
Apart from the more standard fare, richer Romans ate strange and innovative foods such as peacock and nightingale tongues, snails, geese, dormice, ducks, pheasants, pigeons, thrushes, finches, and wild game such as boar and deer. Wealthy Roman parties were often festivals of innovation to see who could produce the most outlandish dishes.

Food for the Poor
Poorer Romans tended to eat what they could find, which was usually ground meal made of different types of grain, and a dish called *puls*. This was a dish made with ground wheat and water. They tended to eat bread and vegetable soup, cheese, fruit, and olives. Meat was a rarity unless they could go hunting for it. While they did drink wine, it was more out of necessity, and there was a distinct lack of experimentation in their diets.

Ways of Cooking
Uncovered Ancient Roman kitchens within the

ruins of Pompeii showed what Roman cooking was once like. Romans cooked their food over specially made long troughs in which flaming hot coals were placed. Meat, fish, vegetables, and poultry were laid on grills over the troughs in order to cook. Stews were cooked in large open pots over fires. The pots were mounted on tripods over the fire (Mandal, 2016).

Roman Jobs

Romans had many different kinds of occupations throughout the empire. Manpower was needed to keep the order and structure of daily life running and to maintain the stability of the empire.

Many Roman citizens were farmers. Their job was vital, as they had to prepare and harvest crops with which to feed civilians and the military. They harvested wheat, barley, fruits and vegetables. Wheat, the most common crop, was used to make bread and other baked goods.

Rome had the sturdiest military in the ancient world. It was made of brave men who risked their lives in battle. The military was made of poorer people who wanted to earn a livable wage. Anyone could enlist the Roman army if they were over the age of 17 and were physically fit enough to handle the hardships.

Merchants were the people who were responsible for

the sale of goods and services. They operated in open air markets and were responsible for keeping the economy stable and strong. They sold all manner of goods from weapons and armor, to food, fabrics, linens, dishes, currency, and many more.

Craftsmen were the people responsible for producing the goods sold by merchants. They did all the small jobs people didn't want to do or were too busy. They made pots and dishes, jewelry, swords, leather goods, baskets, art and toys, musical instruments, and many other objects that were of use to people. Some honed their skills in a particular area like making clothes or mending shoes. Either way, they were vital to the expansion of the empire because they fulfilled the small roles that people didn't often see.

Musicians and entertainers were essential to the lifeblood of the empire because they kept people entertained and distracted. They took many forms. Some played music in the streets. Some were tasked with entertaining emperors and people in positions of authority. Others were more skilled at playing certain kinds of musical instruments or at using their bodies to entertain, shock and amuse. Either way, they added color and spice to life throughout the empire.

Lawyers, teachers, and engineers were the intellectual hub of the empire. They often occupied positions of power and had high status roles in finance and legal positions. Teachers were tasked with educating the younger generation and those wanting to further themselves in specific disciplines. Engineers were tasked with designing and developing more efficient transport networks, bridges, roads, and buildings. Lawyers were excellent orators and philosophers and were tasked with giving legal counsel.

Government consisted of the most wealthy and powerful men and women in society. This included rulers, emperors, Senate leaders, judges, wealthy public speakers, orators, governors, and all those in positions of authority within the empire. Many other kinds of people were required in the more complex jobs in order to keep the empire running smoothly such as bankers, tax collectors, creditors, debtors, clerks, and many more. Senators were considered some of the most important people in society.

A Typical Day

Life in the City
Most Romans in the city would start their day by waking up at first light, washing and doing their ablutions, and then sitting down to whatever breakfast happened to be available at the time. Then they would go about their daily work, whatever that hap-

pened to be. They would work until the early afternoon and then have a light meal which would keep them going until *cena*. After their afternoon meal, they would head off to social activities or to the local baths. The evening *cena* was an event that most Romans looked forward to as it gave them a chance to relax from the activities of the day and to communicate with family and friends. Life in the city was marked by a cycle of social life mixed with business and tending to one's friends and family. Community was important to city Romans. A lot of the wealthier people tended to live in the city as well, which made it easier to connect with people of a higher status.

Life in the Country
Daily life in the country was dictated to by what needed to be done and the basic needs of people. Their livelihoods determined what they needed to do each day and how much time they had for the daily tasks that had to be done such as eating and taking care of themselves. One imagines that daily life in the country would begin at the crack of dawn with doing their daily chores and then sitting down to breakfast, which would be simple fare. Farmers worked about seven days a week and rarely got time to take a break, depending on the season. Farmers enjoyed fishing, hunting, riding, and many other outdoor activities that might not have been possible if they were staying in the city. Wealthier Romans who lived in the countryside might have gone for walks, rode horses, and visited with friends who

were staying at nearby villas.

Family

Family structure was important to the Romans. Wives were generally treated with respect and had a say over the finances and the running of the household. Fathers were referred to as *paterfamilias* and were responsible for earning money in their various trades to keep the family strong and stable. They were seen as the head of the *domum* or house. Children in wealthy families had the best education money could buy, while those who were not wealthy would have to be educated at home.

School
The kind of education most families could afford depended on their social status and financial position. The wealthier could attend more expensive schools and later on, specialized classes in order to improve in a specific discipline or trade. Many of the tutors within the system were freedmen or slaves. The school systems used in Rome itself were implemented throughout the empire in order to build a consistent educational culture. That is to say, the same ideas were taught everywhere. Some of these educational systems still hold sway to this very day, such was their quality.

Roman schools were tiny, with only one room and

a single teacher or tutor. Schools were divided into both boys and girls. There were no desks, and only the teacher was allowed to sit on a chair with a back. Reading, writing, speaking, mathematical systems, military history, simple geography, and many other important subjects were taught. It was important for students to learn about the glory of the empire itself and to be educated in the Roman way of law, order, and discipline in whatever field they chose to study. Children from wealthier families were educated privately, and this was often a lot more expensive as the tutors or teachers were trained more thoroughly in their specific disciplines. An emphasis seems to have been placed on speaking well, as this is the stated goal in analyzing many Ancient Roman historical records. Overall, the system was influenced by Grecian practices that the Romans had learned from observing the Hellenic culture. As with many societies, those on the bottom of the Roman social pyramid or those who were poorer had to educate themselves at home and could not afford the very best in education. The Roman way of life and Roman culture was embodied within their educational systems; children were taught about the values that they needed to know growing up so that they could become effective men and women serving in the empire in whatever role they were required to.

Clothing

Roman clothing depended vastly on the occasion of

the day. For those attending special or celebratory events, sophisticated dress was worn. The toga was most commonly worn for public use. The more ornate versions were worn at formal events and by those in positions of authority. They were difficult to wear and in later years within the empire, the tunic with a cloak was preferred as it was more comfortable overall. Depending on the weather, the tunic could be removed if it was too hot or put on if it was cold. Tunics were like a form of shirt that could be worn by rich and poor alike, but they were mostly favored by the poor. Most Romans wore sandals but there are records of more elaborate footwear amongst the more wealthy.

Entertainment
Entertainment was important to both the Roman people and to the Roman government as a whole. According to *Roman Entertainment* (n.d), the government knew that if people were unoccupied, they would cause trouble, so they made great efforts to try and appease the masses by providing different outlets for amusement around the city. These forms of entertainment were mostly free. Most notable amongst these was of course the Colosseum where people watched all kinds of combat, executions, chariot races, recreations of naval battles, and many other often violent activities.

The Circus Maximus was a noted public entertainment venue where people could watch chariot races, gladiatorial fights, and other sporting events.

The Campus was a converted military base on the banks of the Tiber that was used for sports and recreation. Men from all over Rome competed in wrestling tournaments, javelin, archery, boxing, and many other kinds of shows where they could exercise their physical prowess.

There were many other activities for people to take part in such as going to museums to view Roman art, visiting the baths, going to zoological gardens to view rare and interesting animals, and many others.

CHAPTER 5: MYTHOLOGY

Roman mythology refers to the body of stories that make up the origins of the Roman Empire. It refers to the creation of Rome, their gods and goddesses, mythical creatures, aspects of culture, the rationale for Roman beliefs, and deals with the existential elements of how the Roman Empire came to be and what their purpose or positioning was in the world. Rome was a complex and multilayered society whose place in the world was seen as a dominant force. She was both the oppressor and the law-giver. What people believed about Rome affected the way that they acted and carried themselves in public life, in their daily lives and in battle.

The Mythological Origin Of Rome

It is worth noting that Romans were proud of their legends and tales about the empire. They took pride in the fact that these stories existed and passed them down through generations in both written and verbal mediums.

Roman Gods

Roman gods were divided up into the major and minor deities. Each god represented a different aspect of Roman society and culture. Every facet of Roman life was represented in these gods. Before the advent of Christianity in Rome, it was an exclusively Pagan society. The gods themselves were characters within Roman history, and much of the influence on Pagan Rome came from the influences of the surrounding Greek culture.

Jupiter was the alpha Roman god who controlled everything. He was the king of all the Roman gods, and his equivalent in the Greek culture was Zeus. He could summon thunder and lightning like Zeus.

Juno was the Roman equivalent of Hera. She was Jupiter's wife and was considered Rome's protector. She was the queen of all the gods and held great power within the pantheon.

Mars was the Roman god of war. He was also the son of Jupiter and Juno. He was the leader of the military legions and also the agricultural guardian initially. He changed to his familiar warlike role later on and was second only to Jupiter in terms of his power amongst the pantheon of gods.

Venus was the Roman goddess of love, beauty, and romance. She also represented all aspects of sexual desire, lust, fertility, prosperity, and victory. Additionally, she was the goddess of fields and gardens.

Mercury was the god of trade and industry. He is portrayed as being fleet of foot and is synonymous with speed, fertility, luck, and prosperity. Popular sculptures of Mercury have him with wings on his heels, which suggests he also fulfilled the role of the messenger of the gods.

Neptune was the god of the sea. He was the patron of horses and the brother of Jupiter. Before the Romans became a sea-going people, Neptune was confined to being a god of the rivers and streams. It is an example of how perspectives of cultural deities can change over time. As people understood more about their environment, they worshipped their gods in different ways.

Apollo was the god of music, arts and culture, and prophecy and was brother of Diana. He also inspired medicine, health, vitality, and well-being.

Diana was the goddess of hunting, skill, and archery. She also represented animals and living creatures that could be hunted.

Minerva was the goddess of wisdom. She was a parallel of the Greek goddess Artemis.

Ceres was the goddess of agriculture and the harvest. She also represented the climates and seasons. It is from her name that we get the modern term "cereal," which is often a food product made with harvested items such as grain and other similar items.

Vulcan was the Roman god of fire. He was also commonly associated with forging and metalwork.

Bacchus was the Roman god of wine and orgies. He also represented the Roman theatre. Bacchus was associated with fertility, too. The Romans had many fertility gods and would pray and make sacrifices before the harvests were sown in order that they might be more productive and fruitful before the harvest season.

The greatest of the Roman gods was actually Caesar himself. A group calling themselves the Imperial Cult made the worship of Caesar, starting with Julius Caesar, their number one priority. All of the Roman emperors were worshipped except the evil or morally corrupt ones. As the empire grew and developed, emperor worship became formalized. The Roman Emperors of course encouraged this worship as this made their subjects easier to rule and less likely to revolt. On the opposite side of things, if an emperor became unpopular, they were less likely to be viewed as a god and they were more likely to be assassinated and killed as a result.

The character of the Roman deities reflects different aspects of Roman society and even the different personalities of the Roman Emperors themselves. From the more warlike gods to the more peaceful ones, it is clear that the nature of these gods were based on real life people and their personalities in specific cultural moments. One could say that Roman gods were really more like deified men.

Other Cultural Myths

As in many other cultures, the Romans believed in a natural order of things. They believed in gods and goddesses that ruled over various aspects of the natural world and over Roman life. There was a great deal of interest in the supernatural. Pagan Rome was all that existed before the advent of Christianity during the time of Constantine the Great. Roman culture and belief were also heavily influenced by the cultures around at the time, particularly the Grecian or Hellenic culture. Even the structure of their pantheon of gods was similar with many Roman gods being parallels of their Greek equivalent.

Heroism was a common trait within Roman folklore and mythology. It carried over into Romans' real life adventures as well. Romans were expected to be able to cope with all kinds of situations. There was a great deal of emphasis placed on strength and ability, as well as intellectual capability. What follows are some accounts of Roman heroes as they appeared in different parts of literature. Each story is part of the broader tapestry that helps us to understand the Roman Empire and how it functioned. We understand the empire better when we see these stories both individually and collectively.

The story of Aeneas was told in many forms of Roman literature including the Iliad by Homer and

The Aeneid by Virgil. Aeneas was a Roman and Trojan hero who was also the ancestor of Romulus and Remus. After Troy was defeated, Aeneas fled to Rome carrying several statues of Trojan gods which he planted in Italy. He then came into contact with Dido, the queen of Carthage and they fell in love. It was Dido's intention that they rule over the city of Carthage together but Venus, the goddess of love caused their relationship to break up.

To honor his late father, Aeneas arranged a series of funeral games in the gladiatorial style. When he was killed during the games, he descended down into the underworld and met his father and Dido. Aeneas found out from his father what the line of succession in Rome would be. Thus, the line of kings and emperors was established. This story was a favorite of Roman orators over the centuries and it was retold from generation to generation.

The Romans liked to use examples from nature in order to tell their stories. One such example is called "Jupiter and the Bee." This story carries a moral lesson about vengeance and how dangerous it can be to have a vengeful attitude.

One day, after humans had taken away the honey from inside her hive, the queen of all the bees grew enraged. She decided to pay a visit to Jupiter and offered him fresh honey. He was so delighted at the taste of the honey that he offered to give her anything she wished. She asked him only for a stinger that she could use to harm and kill any mortal that tried to approach her hive. Jupiter was annoyed with her request because he loved the human race and did not want to see them suffer. However, he also did not want to deny her request after having promised her something. So he ended up giving her a stinger in her tail which, while wounding the mortal that came near her, would also result in her death. The moral of the story is do not wish for that which can kill you. Rather, forgive.

Apollo is one of the most well known gods in the Roman pantheon. He appears in both Grecian and Roman mythology. Apollo had fallen in love with the beautiful daughter of King Priam. In order to bind her to himself, Apollo promised her the gift of prophecy if she would agree to his wishes. Upon their union, she immediately reneged on their deal, causing Apollo to burst into flames. Enraged, he cursed her so that no one should believe her prophecies. As a result of this, no one believed what she had to say about the Greeks invading the Trojans, and they were destroyed as a result.

A priestess called Io was one of the lovers of the mighty Jupiter, and in order to be closer to her, Jupiter made himself into a dark cloud so that he could hide his activities from his wife Juno. But Juno, being too wise, saw through the disguise. Jupiter then descended to earth and disguised Io as a white cow so as to protect her. Juno discovered the cow and placed it under the care of Argus, a god with 100 eyes. In order to rescue Io, Jupiter sent his son

Mercury to Argus in order to bore him to sleep with many stories. When Mercury was successful in freeing Io, Juno became enraged and sent a large poisonous fly to sting Io for eternity. Only when she vowed never to pursue Jupiter again was Io set free and departed to go to Egypt where she was worshipped as a goddess.

Pluto was named after the Roman god of death. The Roman process of death itself is that one has to cross the river Styx where they pay the undead ferryman with coins that they are buried with. The coin has to be inside the mouth of the person being ferried or the ferryman, Charon, will not transport them. The river was considered bad news to even the strongest gods. Anyone coming into contact with it would lose their voice for nine whole years. As an aside, the Greek god of death, or the underworld, was called Hades. As you can tell, the Greeks and Romans had many parallels in their culture.

One of the greatest Roman and Greek heroes of all time was the mighty Heracles, or Hercules. He was considered to be half man and half god, and was capable of feats of extraordinary strength. He was capable of wrestling with and overcoming supernatural beings of extraordinary strength. One of the most popular stories surrounding Hercules, or Heracles, is the legend of the twelve tasks. He had to perform these tasks in order to appease the goddess Hera, or Juno in Roman lore.

Janus was the Roman god of beginnings and endings. He had two faces, signifying the past and the future. He was responsible for the changes in times and seasons. In Roman mythology, there is a story about a woman who was captured by Romulus and had to be rescued. Janus saved the woman and drowned the kidnappers under hot lava. He was in control of the natural world and all the elements.

Paganism In Ancient Rome

Paganism in Ancient Rome lasted up until the advent of Christianity under Emperor Constantine the Great who outlawed all such practices. In the 4th century, he began to remove all traces of Pagan objects from the Roman Senate house and from the temples themselves. All traces of Pagan Rome were eventually stripped away to make way for a more Christianized Rome. But, what was the nature of Paganism in Rome? What did people believe? It's important to see how Paganism had an impact on their daily lives. How did their beliefs lead to the myths that we know today?

Paganism involved the worship of the natural world and the observable universe around the Roman Empire. People had to make sense of what they saw, and they invented stories to do it. Gaps in the Roman oral tradition were filled in by influences from other cultures, and this is evident when studying Ancient Roman literature and the stories that were handed down for generations.

CHAPTER 7: ROMAN MILITARY

The Roman army was the strongest of its time. With capable military leaders, sophisticated weapons and tactics, and a motivated and disciplined force, they were the strongest fighting force of their age and time period. This fighting force enabled the Romans to maintain control of the known ancient world for many hundreds of years. What made the Roman army different from other armies at the time? What weapons, tactics, and strategies did they employ that made them the envy of the world? The Roman army was a reflection, in many ways, of the nature of the empire itself. When it was strong, Rome was strong. When it was divided, fragmented, and leaderless, it showed in the way that the empire was being governed. It was an inseparable part of the strength and glory of the empire.

Structure

The Roman army was made up of smaller and larger units. The smaller units were known as cohorts. Cohorts fit together into the larger structure known as legions, which will be addressed in more detail later. Each legion had 59 governing centurions. A cohort was made up of about 480 men. There was one centurion for every 80 men within a cohort.

Each legion had around 120 *alae* or cavalry. These units were also known as belonging to the unit *Eques Legionis.* They were used not as heavy cavalry, but as reconnaissance troops and units for harassing enemy supply chains. They were also utilized as messengers that could quickly and quietly slip through enemy lines or between outposts to deliver news or important information.

Each centurion, cohort, and legion had its own symbol, banner, and a flag which was held up on a long pole. These were carried into battle.

The commanding officer of a legion was called a legate or *Legatus Legionis.*

Logistics

The Roman army was known for its supreme discipline and fortitude. They had to make forced marches, sometimes as much as 20 miles or 30 kilometers a day, carrying heavy sacks on their backs. When they were in the field, they had to handle not only their weapons and armor, but also their clothes, pots and pans, and other cooking utensils. They carried everything they needed in order to survive in the field. According to *The Roman Army* (n.d), the Romans would share a tent while in the field. While on the move, mules were used to move heavy loads such as the tents and other large packs that would have weighed the infantry down. While the Roman soldiers themselves were sturdy enough, carrying too much weight would have slowed the entire advance of the army, and thus pack animals were used for a large portion of the work.

Depending on the conditions of battle and who and where they were fighting in the world, the Romans would make extensive use of conscripts who had better knowledge of the terrain than they did. These auxiliaries were paid less than the Roman soldiers themselves, but also received other rewards for their service; they were offered the opportunity to become Roman citizens once the war was over. To become a Roman citizen in those days was a huge reward for any man, as it brought with it a host of privileges.

Under the command of a Roman Emperor Gaius Marius, the Roman army was reformed and became even more battle-hardened in around 100 BC. Roman soldiers were often referred to as "Marius mules" due to the amount of equipment they had to carry. Such equipment included their food, weapons, rope, sickles, shield, pick-axe, and many other items that were needed in battle and in the field. The men also had to travel long distances in a day. It was a test of endurance. Roman soldiers would march, fight, build bridges, and break into fortresses, sometimes all in one day. At the end of the day, the camp consisting of heavy wooden logs had to be built, and trenches had to be dug around the perimeter. In the morning, it had to be uprooted again.. This all was arduous and back- breaking work. Punishments were often harsh for soldiers who fell asleep or who broke the rules.

Legions

The Roman army consisted of two groups: auxiliaries and legionaries. Legionaries were soldiers younger than 45. Auxiliaries were soldiers who were not Roman citizens, conscripted from other tribes. Rome had conquered many territories and had a lot of manpower if they needed additional soldiers for their military forces. Each legion consisted of ten cohorts. The first cohort consisted of 800 men and the other nine consisted of 480 men each.

Training

A Roman soldier was a trained fighting machine, equipped to deal with the most extreme of battle situations. Only men were allowed to enlist in the army, and those who were under the age of 17 or were too weak or physically unfit were rejected. A term of about 25 years in the army was the standard contract for most Roman soldiers. If they survived their time, they were rewarded with gifts of land, and they were allowed to retire in peace. Older soldiers sometimes lived together in towns called *colonia*. Training itself lasted for about four months. Soldiers were put through a series of tests. If they failed, they would be put onto specific diets or receive specific kinds of training.

The army education was divided up into individual training, collective training, as well as combat and non-combat training (survival). Individual training was all about whether the soldier could keep themselves fit and mentally alert. This also included practice with both melee and ranged weapons. The soldiers were put through a range of physical exercises every day which included swimming, jumping, running, lifting heavy objects, and other kinds of physical activity.

Collective training dealt with the tactical aspects of warfare and understanding how to work as a group. Roman soldiers did not train solely for the purposes of improving their physical condition or to improve morale, or for collective pride and belief. They trained because they knew that they were going to go into real-life situations and they would need to employ the skills that they were learning. The reality of life in the Roman Empire was often savage and cruel, and they needed to be prepared. Aspects of collective training included how to march and parade as a unit, keeping their rank and file, and how to construct military buildings, palisades, and dig ditches. They would have practice fights against members of their own units with wooden swords. These fights would be to see who could dislodge the other unit's formation first.

Every so often, infantry and cavalry would go on route marches together. These were tests to see who could apply their skill while they were out in the field. There was no combat involved, but was still rigorous. It allowed the soldiers to put into practice what they had learned: camping drills, building exercises, and crossing rivers. The cavalry would also undertake the maneuvers they had learned while at the school.

Large scale military drills were also practiced, and it was not uncommon to receive a visit from the emperor himself on occasion. Hadrian was one of the emperors most noted for visiting troops in the field and on the frontline. He gave praise, criticism, and remarked on the training and discipline of the troops.

Training Infrastructure
Roman soldiers lived and trained in tents for the most part. To ensure that training was done correctly, the proper buildings needed to be in place. Training was usually conducted outside, but in the case of rainy or inclement weather, it could be moved indoors if necessary.

There were different kinds of camps for differing

units and various kinds of training. There were areas for training on how to build bridges and forts; there were siege workshops, ranges for practicing archery and artillery maneuvers, and there were areas where infantry formations could be practiced. This meant that Roman training camps tended to be very large and established institutions. They were expensive to maintain and were considered to be well-respected.

There were many kinds of people running these camps. For example, there were *campidoctores*, or drill instructors, whose job it was to ensure that the standards of the troops never dropped. A *doctor armorum* was considered to be an expert in the use of weaponry of all kinds. A *doctor cohortis* was the drill instructor for an entire platoon or cohort. They specialized in larger scale maneuvers. *Exercitatores* or *magister campi* were the specialists in cavalry related moves and formations.

Romans Soldiers In Everyday Life

Roman soldiers weren't only used for fighting. They had many practical advantages outside of the military. Soldiers could be used to build entire cities and structures. They helped with the building of roads, schools, bridges, encampments, and many other types of structures. When on the front line, the infantry who were building towers and military outposts were often guarded by the cavalry.

Benefits of Roman Army Training
Some historians have noted that the training that the Romans went through really helped soldiers when they were on the field of battle. Being in the outdoors constantly prepared the Roman soldiers for the reality of battle and for long, drawn-out campaigns. Being constantly tired, thirsty, and hungry while having to face extreme conditions was enough to acclimatize them for the conditions they had to face in the theatre of war. Constant exercises with other soldiers helped to build up a sense of camaraderie between the troops. This bond between Roman soldiers made them a more effective fighting unit in the heat of battle. The understanding that they had and the friendships that they built while in the field were effective motivators. The mental and physical resiliency that they had built up while doing their training could sometimes be the deciding factor in swaying close battles.

Navy

Initially, up until around the 3rd century, the Roman army was not noted for being a naval civilization. Their prowess on land was usually enough to crush the armies of most civilizations, but they tended to struggle as soon as they got onto the open ocean. However, over time, this changed. During the first

Punic war in around 264 BC, they came up against a fantastically organized naval power in Carthage, and this proved to be the catalyst for their embracing of naval strategy. Up until this point, Carthage had been the world power when it came to ocean-going endeavors. The Romans knew that this would have to change if they were going to consolidate the power that they had won. In order to overcome Carthage, Rome would need to rebuild their navy from scratch, build harbors, and learn the basics of naval warfare. It was a momental ask.

To begin, Rome tried to level the playing field by making use of its greatest strength at sea: the infantry. In order to engage the enemy at sea, the Romans invented the aforementioned *corvus*, a device that enabled the infantry to get across a flat platform in order to attack enemy troops on their ships. Unfortunately the *corvus* did have some drawbacks, namely the fact that it could not be used on rough seas due to its inflexible nature. It would cause more damage to both ships than was necessary. In an age where ship building was expensive and time-consuming, the Romans could not afford to lose so many vessels. Over time, the *corvus* was phased out and replaced with more efficient ancient warfare tactics. By the time the *corvus* had disappeared from use, the Roman army was already a highly effective naval superpower and had no further use for it.

During the imperial period of Roman history, there were no enemies left to fight save for a few pirate raids which were easily dealt with, although they were a nuisance. For the most part, the Roman navy was only used to transport grain and industrial materials without seeing anything of war.

Weapons And Tactics

Weaponry

Roman soldiers used a great variety of weapons on the field of battle. Which weapons were preferred depended on the nature of the battle. If it was a siege, siege equipment would be used to crack open stubborn enemy cities. If a defensive wall was needed, more armored troops would be called into play. According to *Ancient Rome: Roman Army* (n.d), Romans soldiers used a variety of different kinds of weapons including daggers, short swords, spears (for thrusting), javelins, and (depending on their station) a bow and arrow as well. The Roman short sword, or the gladius, proved effective in close quarters of battle and enabled them to destroy the Grecian army during their invasion and occupation of Greece. The short sword was cheap and efficient to manufacture, and it offered improved mobility, although it was not a substitute for heavier forms of weaponry of course.

Roman siege equipment was amongst the best in the world. The siege weapons they developed were adapted from what they learned from the Hellenic siege culture in the early years of the empire. The siege weapons the Roman army used included the *ballista,* the onager, the battering ram, *scorpio*, and various kinds of artillery. There were also Roman siege divisions tasked with designing, constructing, and operating the siege equipment, digging underneath walls, and planning the strategy for invading fortified towns.

Siege Equipment

One of the most well-known tools that the Roman army used was the battering ram. It was a large, heavy, wheeled beam-like construction that was covered with sheets of iron to make it as heavy as possible. Men inside the ram would push it into enemy structures (while remaining safe from enemy arrow fire). It was used on slow-moving and stationary targets.

Another effective Roman weapon was the *ballista*. It was a form of ancient artillery that could launch large projectiles, bolts, or arrow-like weapons at masses of units. It was considered to be extremely accurate on the battlefield. The *ballista* was a fixed construction on the ground which was operated by drawing a drawstring back and letting it go, much the same as would have happened with a bow and arrow. They were made use of by Julius Caesar during his battles in Britain and during the battle in Gaul at Alesia.

Siege towers were large, tall, wheeled structures that could be used to aid infantry and soldiers in accessing walls and other towers. They gave a bird's eye view of the battle and offered the advantage of height to troops that were in the tower. Arrows, rocks, and other projectiles could be launched from these towers, and they were also resistant to archer fire. Siege towers contained structures which could raise or lower them to the height of the wall if it was required. They were used at the siege of Masada in 74 AD and at the siege of Yodfat in 67 AD, amongst other campaigns.

Mines were tunnels that were dug under enemy fortifications such as walls and towers. They also weakened the walls and caused structures to collapse or made them easier to knock down. Special teams of engineers called sappers created tunnels filled with resin, sulfur, and incendiary materials in order to destroy these tunnels and whatever structures happened to be on the ground above them. The use seemed to be a specific Roman tactic and a terrifying one for people inside the cities who could hear the Romans slowly but surely advancing underneath them, while the battle raged outside.

In naval battles, the Roman army made use of something known as a *corvus* in order to board enemy ships. It was a siege engine but it was also a plank-like bridge with a spike in it that was affixed to a Roman vessel via a pole. The plank could be raised or lowered by a series of pulleys, and when it was dropped on the deck of an enemy ship, the spike would embed itself in the deck of that ship and was impossible to remove. Once the ships were latched together, they could not be maneuvered properly, nor could they be disentangled easily. Roman soldiers could then board the opposing ship and set fire to it or slaughter the people on board. Soldiers would advance on the opposing ship with their shields in front of them to avoid being struck by enemy projectiles or swords.

The *scorpio* was a device that looks like a crossbow with wheels on either side. It could be moved into position using these wheels. They were an anti-personnel weapon rather than a weapon that could break down fortifications. *Scorpio* were easier to move into position than ballistae or similar types of weapons, due to their smaller size. But even though they were small, they were still able to do major damage to armored troops.

Onagers or catapults were large, heavy, wheeled, projectile-throwing weapons that could launch weighty objects long distances. They were intended for firing on masses of units causing widespread destruction. But their primary purpose was for destroying walls and fortifications that would otherwise be impervious to other siege weapons. The projectiles that they launched were large rocks or heavy objects doused in a flammable material and set on fire.

Tactics

The Roman way of operating was to dominate the battlefield and to control the outcome of battle. Romans would advance into the midst of battle under the cover of their shields in order to protect themselves from enemy archer fire. Their defense was strong, and they counterattacked the enemy from their fortified position. The Roman army had many different shield formations that they used depending on the situation they found themselves in. These formations could be adjusted during the course of a battle so that they could gain the advantage. One of the most common Roman military maneuvers was known as the *testudo*. This was a formation that was based on a tortoise's shell; the formation itself was designed to protect the soldiers inside from enemy fire. Soldiers held their shields over their heads and crouched inside the formation or block while advancing or holding a defensive position.

Another popular formation was the wedge. It was created to drive at enemy formations and break them open; thereafter, the Roman soldiers would create havoc inside enemy lines and destroy them. Legionaries would form a triangle-shaped formation and charge the enemy with their gladiuses drawn.

Initially, the Romans had employed the phalanx formation themselves during the early years of the empire. This was a formation that required soldiers to move forward as a unified block and to throw the enemy off balance by counter punching their way to victory. It was popularized in Hellenic culture and was taken forward by these early Roman armies. The long-handled spears were most effective in this formation at driving into the enemy lines and breaking them apart while being very defensively rigid. However, the Romans discovered in their battles against the more nimble Samnites that this formation wasn't so effective on terrain that was more rocky; and thereafter, they modified the way that they handled combat.

When the Romans did eventually meet the Greeks in battle during the wars 146 BC, they came up against the phalanx themselves and trounced it. A new brand of warfare had come to the ancient world based on mobility and speed, rather than relying solely on heavy armor. The Roman's ability to utilize their short swords in small spaces completely confused the Greeks heavier, but slower armored units. They were cut to pieces in a short time during these wars. The Romans introduced the idea of infantry being organized into small groups depending on their function within the battle. Each unit functioned as part of the larger whole. The names of these groups were: *velites, hastati, principes,* and *triarii.*

Velites were young and inexperienced soldiers

whose role was to hold the front line of the Roman army as they marched into battle. They were meant to press the enemy early on in battle. When they were recalled after the first phase of the battle was over, they returned to the front line and the next zone or group of Roman soldiers took their place. These were known as the *hastati*. These men were responsible for the next phase of action: the javelin phase. When they were about 35 yards or 32 meters from the enemy, they stood with their javelins facing towards the opposition. When their commander gave the order, they threw their javelins at the enemy, injuring or killing those in the front line or disabling enemy cavalry. Once they had launched their javelins, they rushed towards the opposition with their swords ready while the soldiers behind them threw their javelins over their own heads and into the ranks of the enemy. If the charge of the *hastati* was unsuccessful, they would reform at the back of the column and the next phase of Roman soldiers would take their place: the *principes*. As the name implies, these were the best soldiers that the empire had to offer. They were often the most skilled and made their presence felt on the battlefield when the enemy was disorganized and ravaged from the previous two attacks. If the previous attacks were unsuccessful, historical records indicate that this was usually the attack that completely routed the enemy. If for some reason the enemy was more resilient than usual, the *principes* would be withdrawn and the next and final phase of the column would be brought to the front to engage the enemy, the *triarii*. These were usually the heaviest of the infantry and the unit was made up of older and wealthier men. They were usually the last resort when the Roman army had exhausted its first three options.

If the enemy retreated, Roman cavalry would be brought up. While the Romans were not a noted cavalry civilization, they still made extensive use of these units in order to ensure that they were not outflanked by the enemy. Once the danger had passed or the enemy had fled or been routed, the cavalry would be brought up to mop up what remained of the enemy. As previously noted, the Romans were not naturally drawn towards the use of cavalry, a fact which would become significant later on during the final years of the empire's history. However, during the majority of their history, the cavalry units in the Roman army were made up of more skilled conscripts from North Africa and Gaul, according to *Military Tactics of the Roman Army* (n.d).

The Romans paid careful attention to how their cavalry was stationed or where they decided to fight their battles. If the battles were against strong cavalry-oriented armies, the Romans tried to lure the enemy onto rough or mountainous terrain. They also tended to prefer fighting with the wind instead of against it. Launching of projectiles was made more effective depending on which way the wind was blowing and what the speed of the wind was.

As previously mentioned, the Romans made effective use of siege tactics to break down stubborn enemies. Such tactics also included the filling in of defensive ditches with soil or concrete. They would make use of battering rams to weaken the defensive structure of a wall and they also made use of wooden beams with hooks on the end. These hooks would be used to yank the mortar and bricks out of a wall to terminally weaken it and cause it to collapse or to create breaches that Roman troops could pour through into the city. To protect themselves while going into the breach, the Roman troops would make use of the *testudo*. The Romans also invented a kind of crane that could lift groups of men up and over the wall to attack specific enemy positions.

Famous Battles

Rome saw many battles over the years. Some were great victories and others were great defeats. The legacy of these conflicts shaped the world for centuries to come, leading to the extinction of some civilizations, and the birth of others. These battles fundamentally changed the course of human history.

Punic Wars

The Punic wars were some of the most significant land and sea battles fought in the history of the Roman Empire. The battle between Rome and Carthage was between two of the main competing world powers at the time. One such battle was the battle of Cannae, fought near a small village in central Italy. It was considered one of Rome's worst ever defeats. A smaller force of Carthiginians surrounded a much larger force of Roman infantry and cavalry, under the command of Lucius Aemilius and Gaius Terentius Verro, and destroyed them. The scale of Roman life lost equated to the more modern battles of World War 1. So great was the destruction of the Roman army that it was noted as being one of the darkest moments in Roman military history. Out of the 86,000 troops that started the battle, only about 15,000 survived, and these were most reserves.

In the aftermath of this battle, Roman was shaken to the core. They suffered a second massive defeat that year at the battle of Silva Litana but refused to give in to the Carthiginians. They would battle for 14 more years before Rome was finally victorious at the battle of Zama, which would mark the end of Carthiginian superiority and the downfall of their empire.

Teutoburg

This great battle between the Romans and the Germanic people of Saxony and the North Rhine took place in 9 AD in the Teutoburg forest around the Limes Germanicus. It is referred to as the Varian Disaster because it was led by the ill-fated general Publius Quinctilius Varus. The Germanic warriors and their allies ambushed a group of Roman legions and their auxiliaries in the forest while they were marching out of formation on the muddy trails that led into the forest. The Romans seemed to have been taken by surprise. The leader of the Germanic tribe, Arminius, had lived in Rome and knew about Roman tactics and ways of fighting. Because they were so dispersed, the Roman soldiers had little defense against the numerically superior Germanic army and found themselves with little space to maneuver. When they attempted to break out, they walked into a trap at the base of Kalkriese hill with only narrow passages between the mountain passes that they could cross. Without being able to move easily and establish a defensive position, Germanic troops attacked them from above and slaughtered them, leading to the death of Varus and several other Roman army leaders. It turned into a rout for the Roman army. In the aftermath of the battle, the Germanic tribe attempted to cross the Rhine into Gaul but was eventually repelled by the Roman defenses there.

Catalaunian Fields

The battle of the Catalaunian fields was fought in the declining years of the empire, when they were under constant threat of invasion by barbarian tribes. The main figures in this battle were the brilliant young Roman general Flavius Aetius and the barbaric warlord king Attila the Hun. By way of context, Attila had been menacing the western and eastern Roman Empire for many months and sought to take the ownership of Rome for himself by claiming

Honoria, Emperor Valentinian's sister, as his bride. Attila had already attacked large areas in Europe and devastated them. However, the Hunnic way was not to hold territory, but to raid and take what they could, moving on to other areas when they had bled the land dry.

The battle on the Catalaunian fields was one of the last major battles of the western Roman Empire before their eventual collapse in 476. It took place in around 451 AD and was fought between the weakened western Roman Empire's forces and their allies and the ferocious Huns and their own allies. The Roman army was composed largely of auxiliaries and was therefore not at its usual strength. Aetius' regular Roman army was stationed largely in Gaul and was thus rendered largely inoperable at this time. The Roman army started the more aggressive and dominant of the two armies and pushed the Huns back. In the midst of the battlefield was an elevated piece of land that the Huns attempted to take but were beaten to the chase by the Romans. One of the Roman allies' leader, Theodoric the Goth, was killed by a leader of the opposing barbarian tribes.

As night fell, the tide of battle changed slightly, and Aetius became separated from his troops. Not being able to see where they were going in the dark, his ally Thorismund accidentally entered the Hunnic camp while wandering around, and they were ambushed. Fleeing, wounded but still alive, Thorismund withdrew from the battle. The next morning, Aetius and what remained of his Roman and allied forces investigated the battlefield and found it piled high with bodies. Assuming that Attila was low on supplies, Aetius besieged the Hunnic encampment but refused to completely destroy them for fear that he would lose his only bargaining chip in the wars with other barbarian tribes in the future. He withdrew with the outcome of the battle inconclusive and hoped that he had done enough to safeguard the future of Rome. Attila had suffered huge losses. He died two years later in 453 AD, and the Huns ceased to be a serious threat after that. The battle of the Catalaunian fields is considered by many Roman historians to be one of the most violent and brutal conflicts in the history of Roman warfare. It stretched an already depleted western Roman Empire to its breaking point.

Actium
The Roman battle of Actium was a naval battle that took place in around 31 BC, in the final years of the Roman republic. It was fought between the legions of Octavian, or Caesar Augustus, and the forces of Marc Antony who represented Ptolemaic Egypt. Under the command of the skillful general Agrippa, the much smaller force of Octavian was able to overcome the larger force of Antony (about 500 warships to 250). Octavian kept the majority of his ships out of the range of the more effective Ptolemaic warships and as a result, was able to bait them into making a mistake and becoming isolated from one

another. With disorganization present within their ranks, the forces of Marc Antony were made to withdraw.

Corinth

Another amazing battle between the Romans and the Hellenic forces took place at Corinth in 146 BC. This battle was decisive because it led to the ending of the Achaean war and the beginning of Roman hegemony over Greece. In the aftermath of this battle, the Romans completely annihilated Corinth and no part of it is left standing today. A few weeks prior to the battle, the Roman army had destroyed Greek forces at Scarpheia and Boeotia. The battle began when the Grecian forces attacked a Roman encampment containing auxiliaries not expecting an attack from the smaller Greek forces. Because of this carelessness, the Romans were caught by surprise. Their response to this incursion was swift and tragic for the Greeks. The Roman army counterattacked and then faced them on the battlefield outside the city the next day. Initially, the Greek cavalry was able to hold their own lines against the Roman infantry, but when a handpicked brigade of about 1,000 men attacked their flank, they broke ranks and tried to flee back into the city. The Roman army followed and destroyed them as they fled.

In the resulting carnage, the Romans completely ransacked the city of Corinth and destroyed it, leaving no buildings standing.

CHAPTER 8: DECLINE AND FALL OF THE ROMAN EMPIRE

The Beginning Of The End Of The Roman Empire

All empires must eventually draw to an end, or change in some way as the balance of power shifts or the world evolves. New powers rise and grow more rapidly than these empires can manage, or the empires themselves are weakened from within. The Roman Empire was never going to remain as the world's leading power because of the shifts in times and season. All over Europe, other powers were rising. But what led to the eventual fall and disappearance of half of the empire responsible for bringing law and order to the known world for 1,000 years? Such a thing would seem impossible, and yet, it happened.

Factors That Led to the Empire's Decline

Initially, for the first few hundred years of its empire, the Romans had traditionally had the upper hand over the barbarian tribes, especially in Germania and across the Danube and the Rhine. Although they had not had much success in subduing those civilizations completely, they had maintained steady control over these regions and prevented the barbarians from crossing the Rhine. By the 4th century, however, the barbarians had begun to encroach beyond the Roman borders and make inroads into the empire. Although they did not come close to intruding on the empire itself, there were definite warning signs at this point that all was not right within the empire Other barbarian tribes had improved significantly, copying the Roman playbook and developing technologically at a commensurate rate. All of these factors led the opposition north of the Danube to be significantly more troublesome than its predecessors. Combined with a Roman army which did not have the strength of its former legions, it spelled trouble for the Roman Empire as a whole. In 410 AD, the Visigoths sacked the city of Rome, and it was raided again in 455 AD.

Economic troubles also afflicted the Roman Empire right up until it eventually fell and ceased to exist. Increased taxation and rising inflation had led to a widening gap between the haves and the have-nots. In order to escape the rapidly increasing taxation on them, many people who lived in the city fled to the country instead. This led to decreased urban development and the beginnings of urban decay. A reduced labor rate meant Rome had to induct foreign people into its workforce. As they lost territory, they were unable to conscript slave labor in order to keep the empire thriving. They were dealt a further setback in the 5th century when the Vandals claimed North Africa, leading to a further slave shortage. With pirates hindering them on the ocean, supplies and trade were also affected, leading to agricultural concerns and food shortages throughout the empire.

The rise of the eastern Roman Empire was a key factor in the eventual decline of the west, strange as it seems to say. In the 3rd century, the Emperor Diocletian divided the Roman Empire into two halves, western and eastern, claiming that it was too unruly for one person to rule alone. It did make the empire easier to govern, but because they developed at different rates, there was a widening gulf between the more financially wealthy east and the increasingly problematic west. While the east was fortified and guarded carefully, the west was left open to barbarian invasion. Over time, the west became increasingly fragmented and disconnected as one by one, their territories fell.

Over-expansion of the empire eventually led to its weakening. The terrority Rome held sway over was too vast and too difficult to control. Had the Roman Empire settled for a smaller, but more stable empire, it might have stood a better chance against future invasions. Even with the efficient Roman road system, they were unable to effectively communicate with their holdings throughout the empire. Outposts were often too far away from each other to relay important messages in time. This lack of communication meant that if something went wrong, as it often did, help would not be forthcoming for a long time. Local rulers often suffered from rebellions or attacks in their towns. In order to repel the constant stream of invaders which now regularly threatened the peace and stability of the empire, Rome was forced to station troops in these areas and to build defensive fortifications which were often expensive. The increase in military spending led to shortfalls elsewhere in the empire which meant Rome regressed technologically.

Corruption and instability were rampant in the latter years of the empire. An oversized empire was difficult enough to deal with even without ineffective leadership. Once the leadership itself started to weaken, the rest of the empire quickly crumbled. Rome's strength had always been her leadership, and throughout the long years of the empire, this had been what had seen her through numerous challenges. With the leadership gone, the structures underneath them also crumbled. The Roman Senate was most to blame for its culture of excess. Numerous high ranking politicians were regularly being assassinated, and the culture of fear and paranoia led to constant bickering and infighting in all sectors of government. The emperors themselves were often models of wastefulness and excess, and this filtered down through government.

The Huns were considered one of the arch-enemies of Rome during the 5th century. They differed from the other barbarian tribes in that their intention was not to invade and settle, but to raid lands wherever they could and to take what they had stolen back to their own homesteads. They were a nomadic people who reached new strength under the leadership of Attila the Hun, a great warlord and chief of the tribe. They were not the only barbarian tribe vying for control of the Roman peninsula, though. Other tribes were also on the move across Europe in search of new lands, and they crossed paths with the Roman army as they did so. One of these tribes was the Visigoths, who were grudgingly permitted to stay in the Roman Empire. They were treated with extreme cruelty by the Roman soldiers and eventually revolted against Roman rule in the battle of Adrianople in 378 AD. The unprepared Romans negotiated peace with the Goths at that time, but it was broken in 410 AD when Alaric the Goth sacked Rome. At the same time, the Vandals, Gauls, and Saxons were able to take vast swathes of Roman territory.

The rise of Christianity was another critical factor in the weakening of the Roman Empire. When Emperor Constantine the Great legalized Christianity in around 313 AD, it weakened the traditional values that Rome was built on. The Pagan values that they held on to for many years began to fail as a result. Christianity took credit away from the idea that the emperor himself was a god. It eroded trust in the state. Other political actors began to interfere in state affairs, such as the pope and the church. Historians are divided on much Christianity actually contributed towards the decline of the empire. Some feel that it had little impact, while others state that it had a great deal of impact (Andrews, 2019).

The weakening of the Roman military was definitely one of the presiding factors over the fall of the empire. When Rome was prosperous, the government had more and more money to spend on strengthening the military. When the empire started to struggle financially and economically, it also struggled to find enough soldiers to cover the vast spaces of the empire. Rome was forced to employ mercenaries from all over the empire and its other territories. These men were not as loyal or well trained as the Roman soldiers were, and their performance in battle showed as a result. Rome also had many defectors during this time. Many of the barbarians who fought against Rome were once Roman soldiers themselves (Andrews, 2019).

The Timeline For The Decline

When it eventually did happen, the fall of the

Roman Empire was fairly swift, taking place over a period of about 70 years. Although the seeds had long been sown beforehand, when they eventually did produce fruit, it was a quick process. From the period marked as the official end of the western Roman Empire in 476, Roman culture slowly died out over the next 100 years.

The Visigoths sacked Rome in 410 AD after a campaign that lasted for nearly nine years starting in 401 AD. This was one of the first (but not the only) major signs that the Roman Empire was near its end.

From 429 to 435 AD, the Vandals attacked Roman grain supplies in North Africa, leading to a shortage of food in the empire and cutting off a valuable supply line.

From 440 to 454 AD, the Huns attacked and ransacked both the western and eastern Roman Empire. They were paid off in gold from the eastern Roman Empire but they continued to attack and attack until their efforts were thwarted at the battle of the Catalaunian fields in 451 AD. Shortly after that, their ranks fell into confusion.

In 455, the Vandals plundered Rome but they were turned back after a hasty consultation with Pope Leo the First.

The Fall of the Empire in 476

In 476, the empire fell. The ex-Roman barbarian leader Odoacer deposed the last western Roman Empire Romulus Augustulus and established the Kingdom of Italy. What had led up to this was the Vandal invasion of the 50s. When Rome's weaknesses were exposed, other barbarian tribes began to rise up in revolt. Tribes in Gaul, Spain, and other territories began to rebel against what they perceived were their often unjust overlords. At the end of this turbulent process, and through a painful battle of succession, Romulus Augustulus was crowned emperor in 475. Ruling in his son's stead, Romulus' father Orestes made an enemy of an auxiliary general named Odoacer who fomented revolt around the city of Rome and Italy itself. Fleeing to Pavia, Orestes was pursued by the invading barbarian forces and executed. Odoacer was given the title of *patrician* by the Roman Senate, which, fragmented as it was, still held some power. Romulus was sent into exile. Odoacer proclaimed himself king, although not of the whole of Italy, and united the barbarian tribes. He, however, was murdered by an Ostrogoth while enjoying a meal at a banquet in 493 AD. The conqueror of the Roman Empire had been conquered.

Aftermath

The aftermath of the events of 476 was a bloody war of succession over who would take which territories on the Roman peninsula. Odoacer was unable to completely rid Rome of the Ostrogoths who had threatened to overrun it. The eastern Roman

Emperor Justinian fought the Ostrogoth menace for nearly 20 years, eventually overcoming them. The Roman reconquest of the peninsula was halted by the invasion of Italy by the Lombards. Every single territory that the western Roman Empire had won over its 1,000 year history was lost including the British Isles, Greece, North Africa, and many others. All that was left were the territories belonging to the eastern Roman Empire in Anatolia and Turkey. It would continue to exist until 1453, nearly 800 years later. It was overrun by the Ottoman Turkish Empire.

Overall, the western Roman Empire ceased to function as a state and was overrun by tribal invasion after tribal invasion until all traces of its former glory and culture had either been assimilated or ceased to exist.

What followed in the next several hundred years was that the world changed from being one focused on a single world power to being individual territories governing themselves. Never again would the world see such an influential power.

CONCLUSION

Ancient Rome was an empire that grew from nothing on the banks of the Tiber River to become the greatest empire the world has ever seen. Starting as a small town, evolving to a large prosperous city and eventually to a state, then a kingdom, then a republic, and eventually an empire, it continued to grow and grow. The seeds of this growth were found in the adaptability of the people, their solid leadership, and their determination to rise above the difficult circumstances that they found themselves in. They eventually succeeded in making a name for themselves.

The rule of Julius Caesar was the landmark moment between the transition from republic to empire. He was the catalyst that led to the formation of the Ancient Roman world. The development and rise to power of the Roman juggernaut taught us that it is not what you have been given that makes you great, it is what you do with what you have been given. The Roman people made the most of their resources in a way that led to them becoming as powerful as they did.

The Roman military was the greatest standing army

the world has ever seen. Their discipline, courage and resilience has been the inspiration for many fighters who came after them, many thousands of years later when the dust from the empire had long since settled.

The Roman gladiators taught us that self-sacrifice is a prize that no one is exempt from and that no one is too poor to buy. They taught us the value of living and dying nobly. A dignified life and death is not something many aspire to in today's world. The empire was not only the envy of the ancient world, but continues to inspire and educate us even to this day. Countless books, plays, movies, songs, and poems have been written or sung about this glorious period in world history. What studying this period in ancient history has taught us is that every empire has a beginning and an end. Ancient Rome had many problems: corruption, greed, excess, and every kind of evil. It was a great empire, but it was a brutal one. We learned that nothing lasts forever, no matter how strong or solid it may be. Even the greatest empires may crumble if they depart from the principles that made them great. Change is not evil but is a necessary part of life.

The Roman Empire fell in 476 and disappeared, but the lessons they imparted and the legacy that they left behind still exist to this day. One can view the statues of Ancient Roman Emperors and learn from their stories. This book has demonstrated that vast and ancient civilizations are more than just the people who rule over them. They are made and constructed by the people who lived in them. The battles that they fought, in both victory and defeat, are the stuff of legend and continue to bring hope to us even today. The Roman people faced insurmountable odds, at times, in their fight to stay relevant in the ancient era. The people of the Roman Empire were a microcosm of the empire itself: strong, tough, and resilient.

This book has provided the basis for a careful analysis of these people and their role in history. The intention of analyzing these stories and the history behind them was to examine the assumptions up which Ancient Rome was built. It examined the good and the bad, and sometimes even the ugly. From its rise to its end, the most significant parts of what made the Roman Empire special are the times when it inspires us to go beyond what we are capable of doing and to stretch ourselves to heights we never knew were possible. The world's greatest empire teaches us that the limits of human potential are without end when we truly believe that we can do the impossible.

FREE BONUS FROM HBA: EBOOK BUNDLE

Greetings!

First of all, thank you for reading our books. As fellow passionate readers of history and mythology we aim to create the very best books for our readers.

Now, we invite you to join our VIP list. As a welcome gift we offer the History & Mythology Ebook Bundle below for free. Plus you can be the first to receive new books and exclusives! Remember it's 100% free to join.

Simply click the link below to join.

Click Here For Your Free Bonus (https://www.subscribepage.com/hba)

Keep upto date with us on:
YouTube: History Brought Alive
Facebook: History Brought Alive
www.historybroughtalive.com

REFERENCES

Adhikari, S. (2019a, February 11). Top 10 Interesting Roman Mythology Stories. Ancient History Lists. https://www.ancienthistorylists.com/rome-history/top-10-interesting-roman-mythology/

Adhikari, S. (2019b, April 9). Top 10 Famous People in Ancient Rome. Ancient History Lists. https://www.ancienthistorylists.com/rome-history/top-10-famous-people-ancient-rome/

Adhikari, S. (2019, April 29). Top 10 Greatest Emperors of Ancient Rome. Ancient History Lists. https://www.ancienthistorylists.com/rome-history/top-10-greatest-emperors-ancient-rome/

Alexander Hugh McDonald. (2019). Tacitus | Roman historian. In Encyclopædia Britannica. https://www.britannica.com/biography/Tacitus-Roman-historian

Ancient Roman Entertainment. (2020). Wabash. http://persweb.wabash.edu/facstaff/royaltyr/AncientCities/web/bradleyj/Project%201/Games.html#:~:text=Men%20all%20over

%20Rome%20enjoyed

Ancient Roman Recipes. (2000, November). PBS. https://www.pbs.org/wgbh/nova/article/roman-recipes/

Ancient Roman statutes : translation, with introduction, commentary, glossary, and index. (2019). Yale; Austin : University of Texas Press, 1961. https://avalon.law.yale.edu/ancient/twelve_tables.asp

Ancient Rome: Food and Drink. (2019). Ducksters. https://www.ducksters.com/history/ancient_rome/food_and_drink.php

Andrews, E. (2018, August 29). 8 Reasons Why Rome Fell. HISTORY. https://www.history.com/news/8-reasons-why-rome-fell

Arnott, G. (2019). Terence | Roman dramatist | Britannica. In Encyclopædia Britannica. https://www.britannica.com/biography/Terence

Augustus. (2018, August 21). HISTORY. https://www.history.com/topics/ancient-history/emperor-augustus

Battle of Actium. (2021, April 26). Wikipedia. https://en.wikipedia.org/wiki/Battle_of_Actium#Battle

Battle of Cannae. (2020, March 4). Wikipedia. https://en.wikipedia.org/wiki/Battle_of_Cannae

Battle of Corinth (146 BC). (2021, April 9). Wikipedia. https://en.wikipedia.org/wiki/Battle_of_Corinth_(146_BC)#Battle

Battle of the Catalaunian Plains. (2021, April 25). Wikipedia. https://en.wikipedia.org/wiki/Battle_of_the_Catalaunian_Plains#Battle

Battle of the Teutoburg Forest. (2021, April 22). Wikipedia. https://en.wikipedia.org/wiki/Battle_of_the_Teutoburg_Forest#Battles

Beneš, C. E. (2009). Whose SPQR?: Sovereignty and Semiotics in Medieval Rome. Speculum, 84(4), 874–904. https://www.jstor.org/stable/40593680?seq=1

Byzantium: The New Rome. (n.d.). Lumen Learning. https://courses.lumenlearning.com/boundless-worldhistory/chapter/byzantium-the-new-rome/#:~:text=One%20of%20Constantine

Cartwright, M. (2013, October 22). Roman Warfare. World History Encyclopedia. https://www.worldhistory.org/Roman_Warfare/

Cartwright, M. (2014, April 13). Roman Naval Warfare. World History Encyclopedia. https://www.worldhistory.org/Roman_Naval_Warfare/

Cicero. (n.d.). Internet Encyclopedia of Philosophy. https://iep.utm.edu/cicero/#H3

Constantine the Great: History of York.

(n.d.). History of York. http://www.history-ofyork.org.uk/themes/constantine-the-great

Daily Life in the country. (n.d.). Rome. https://rome.mrdonn.org/countrylife.html#:~:text=In%20the%20country%2C%20they%20enjoyed

Dattatreya, M. (2016, August 8). Restored Pompeii Kitchens Glimpses Into Ancient Roman Cooking Styles. Realm of History. https://www.realmofhistory.com/2016/08/08/restored-pompeii-kitchens-roman-cooking/

Deposition of Romulus Augustus. (2020, December 15). Wikipedia. https://en.wikipedia.org/wiki/Deposition_of_Romulus_Augustus

Flavius Aetius. (2021, April 4). Wikipedia. https://en.wikipedia.org/wiki/Flavius_Aetius

Geography of the Roman World. (n.d.). Students of History. https://www.studentsofhistory.com/geography-of-the-roman-world

Greenspan, J. (2018, August 30). 8 Things You May Not Know About Augustus. HISTORY. https://www.history.com/news/8-things-you-may-not-know-about-augustus

Hannibal. (2018, August 21). HISTORY. https://www.history.com/topics/ancient-history/hannibal

Hays, J. (n.d.). MUSIC IN ANCIENT ROME. Facts and Details. http://factsanddetails.com/world/cat56/sub399/entry-6333.html

Hays, J. (2018). GEOGRAPHY AND CLIMATE IN ANCIENT ROME. Facts and Details. http://factsanddetails.com/world/cat56/sub401/item2048.html

History of Ancient Rome for Kids: Roman Food, Jobs, Daily Life. (2018). Ducksters. https://www.ducksters.com/history/ancient_rome_food_daily_life.php

History of Ancient Rome for Kids: Roman Gods and Mythology. (2019). Ducksters. https://www.ducksters.com/history/ancient_roman_gods_mythology.php

History of Ancient Rome for Kids: The Roman Army and Legion. (n.d.). Ducksters. https://www.ducksters.com/history/ancient_rome_army_legions.php#:~:text=The%20Roman%20soldiers%20used%20a

Imperial Roman Army – Training. (2016, April 29). Military History Visualized - Official Homepage for the YouTube Channel. http://militaryhistoryvisualized.com/imperial-roman-army-training/

Julius Caesar. (2017, November 30). Biography; A&E Television Networks. https://www.biography.com/political-figure/julius-caesar

Kemezis, A. (2014). From Antonine to Severan (A. M. Kemezis, Ed.). Cambridge University Press; Cambridge University Press. https://www.

cambridge.org/core/books/greek-narratives-of-the-roman-empire-under-the-severans/from-antonine-to-severan/31AD-C6E1D2C80976502676EEFC264BB4

List of Roman Authors. (n.d.). Latinitium. https://www.latinitium.com/blog/list-of-roman-authors/#3rdcenturyad

Lloyd, J. (2013, April 13). Roman Army. World History Encyclopedia. https://www.worldhistory.org/Roman_Army/

Mark, J. (2008, September 2). Ancient Rome. World History Encyclopedia. https://www.worldhistory.org/Rome/

Marrison, R. (2020, August 24). Top 10 famous Roman Gladiators. History Ten. https://historyten.com/roman/famous-roman-gladiators/

Military Tactics of the Roman Army. (n.d.). Spartacus Educational. https://spartacus-educational.com/ROMmilitary.htm#:~:text=The%20combat%20formation%20used%20by

National Geographic Society. (2018, July 6). Rome's Transition from Republic to Empire. National Geographic Society. https://www.nationalgeographic.org/article/romes-transition-republic-empire/

Paganism and Rome. (2019). University

of Chicago. https://penelope.uchicago.edu/~grout/encyclopaedia_romana/greece/paganism/paganism.html

Pliny the Younger - Ancient Rome - Classical Literature. (n.d.). Ancient Literature. https://www.ancient-literature.com/rome_pliny.html

Ricketts, C. (2018, August 18). 5 Key Works of Roman Literature. History Hit. https://www.historyhit.com/key-works-of-roman-literature/

Roe, I. (2012, January 19). 7 Greatest Roman Generals. Listverse. https://listverse.com/2012/01/19/7-greatest-roman-generals/

Roman Empire. (2020, November 21). Wikipedia. https://en.wikipedia.org/wiki/Roman_Empire#Fall_in_the_West_and_survival_in_the_East

Roman Empire (27 BC – 476 AD) - History of Rome. (2019). Rome. https://www.rome.net/roman-empire

Roman geography. (n.d.). Ancient Roman Civilization. https://galligan18.weebly.com/roman-geographyregionlocation.html#:~:text=Geography%2Flocation

ROMAN MEALS: An Introduction. (n.d.). Carroll. https://www.carroll.edu/sites/default/files/content/academics/philosophy/msmillie/

foodilap/introRommeal.htm

Roman navy. (2021, March 2). Wikipedia. https://en.wikipedia.org/wiki/Roman_navy

Roman Navy - Know the Romans. (n.d.). Know the Romans. https://www.knowtheromans.co.uk/roman-army/roman-navy/

Roman Republic (509 BC – 27 BC) - History of Rome. (2019). Rome. https://www.rome.net/roman-republic

Rome founded. (2019, February 20). HISTORY. https://www.history.com/this-day-in-history/rome-founded

Rome Timeline. (n.d.). World History. https://www.worldhistory.org/timeline/Rome/

Second Triumvirate - Livius. (2003). Livius. https://www.livius.org/articles/concept/triumvir/second-triumvirate/

Septimius Severus. (n.d.). Encyclopedia Britannica. https://www.britannica.com/biography/Septimius-Severus

Simkin, J. (2014). The Roman Army. Spartacus Educational. https://spartacus-educational.com/ROMarmy.htm

Tacitus | Encyclopedia.com. (2018, August 18). Encyclopedia. https://www.encyclopedia.com/people/history/historians-ancient-biographies/tacitus

Tacitus and Jesus. Christ Myth refuted. Did Jesus exist? (n.d.). Tektonics. https://www.tektonics.org/jesusexist/tacitus.php

The Bestiarius and the Ludus Matutinus. (n.d.). University of Chicago. https://penelope.uchicago.edu/~grout/encyclopaedia_romana/gladiators/bestiarii.html

The Geography of Ancient Rome. (n.d.). Scott Devlin. https://sites.google.com/site/romescottdevlin/the-geography-of-ancient-rome

The Geography of Transport Systems. (n.d.). The Geography of Transport Systems. Retrieved April 27, 2021, from https://transportgeography.org/contents/chapter1/emergence-of-mechanized-transportation-systems/roman-empire-c125ce/

The Roman Empire: in the First Century. The Roman Empire. Emperors. Julius Caeser | PBS. (2019). PBS. https://www.pbs.org/empires/romans/empire/julius_caesar.html

The Roman Republic. (n.d.). Khan Academy. https://www.khanacademy.org/humanities/world-history/ancient-medieval/roman-empire/a/roman-republic#:~:text=Rome%20was%20able%20to%20gain

The Roman Tortoise. (2013). Primary Homework Help. http://www.primaryhomeworkhelp.co.uk/romans/formation.html

Tilburg, C. (2019). Via publica. The Encyclopedia of Ancient History, 1–1. https://doi.org/10.1002/9781444338386.wbeah06342.pub2

Trueman, C. N. (2015, March 16). Rome and Christianity. History Learning Site. https://www.historylearningsite.co.uk/ancient-rome/rome-and-christianity/#:~:text=Rome%20had%20a%20large%20number

US history. (n.d.). The Pax Romana. US History. https://www.ushistory.org/civ/6c.asp

US history. (2019). The Fall of the Roman Empire. US History. https://www.ushistory.org/civ/6f.asp

Wasson, D. (2016a, March 20). First Triumvirate. World History Encyclopedia. https://www.worldhistory.org/First_Triumvirate/

Wasson, D. (2016b, April 7). Roman Republic. World History Encyclopedia. https://www.worldhistory.org/Roman_Republic/

What was life like in the Roman army? (2019, November 14). BBC Bitesize; BBC. https://www.bbc.co.uk/bitesize/topics/zwmpfg8/articles/zqbnfg8

Williams, N. (2016, December 16). Geography and Topography of Rome and the Roman Empire. Humanities LibreTexts. https://human.libretexts.org/Bookshelves/History/World_History/Book%3A_World_History_-_Cultures_States_and_Societies_to_1500_(Berger-_et_al.)/06%3A_The_Roman_World_from_753_BCE_to_500_BCE/6.05%3A_Geography_and_Topography_of_Rome_and_the_Roman_Empire

Zoccali, N. (2019, June 20). What is garum? Gourmet Traveller. https://www.gourmettraveller.com.au/recipes/explainers/what-is-garum-17421

Printed in Great Britain
by Amazon